Poppy took her attention off the road to stare at Jake

"You made a note of my *cup size?*" she asked, her voice rising.

"Sure. I'm not blind. All the photos I ever saw, you looked about an A cup. So, what, you stopped training and puberty kicked in, is that it?"

He spoke conversationally. As though it was perfectly natural for him to go around guessing women's breast sizes.

She clenched her hands on the wheel. "We are not talking about my breasts."

"You brought it up."

"I did not! You were staring at me!"

"Because you changed into that teeny, tiny tank. I could hardly pretend I didn't notice."

"The air-conditioning is broken and I was hot and you could've tried! A gentleman would have," she said.

He laughed. "A gentleman? Baby, I'm a journalist. I wouldn't have a job if I was a gentleman."

Blaze

Dear Reader,

What happens when a one-night stand becomes more than it should be? That's the question that was the seed for *Her Secret Fling*. Two consenting adults have a good time and agree that's all it was—then life intervenes and forces them to get to know each other. And, surprise surprise, they like what they discover—after some twists and turns along the way, naturally.

There's a scene toward the beginning of the book that was in my mind from the moment I started imagining this story. I call it "man versus machine," and if you're reading this after finishing the book, you'll know what I'm talking about. If you're reading this letter first... well, you'll know what I'm talking about pretty soon! I hope it tickles your funny bone as much as it did mine.

Most of all, I hope you enjoy reading about Jake and Poppy's story as they work their way around to realizing they need each other and that loving someone is a gift, not a burden. I love to hear from readers, so please drop me a line at sarah@sarahmayberry.com if you feel the urge.

Until next time,

Sarah Mayberry

Sarah Mayberry

HER SECRET FLING

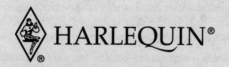

HARLEQUIN®

TORONTO • NEW YORK • LONDON
AMSTERDAM • PARIS • SYDNEY • HAMBURG
STOCKHOLM • ATHENS • TOKYO • MILAN • MADRID
PRAGUE • WARSAW • BUDAPEST • AUCKLAND

Recycling programs
for this product may
not exist in your area.

ISBN-13: 978-0-373-79521-5

HER SECRET FLING

www.eHarlequin.com

Printed in U.S.A.

ABOUT THE AUTHOR

Sarah Mayberry is an Australian by birth and a Gypsy by career. At present she's living in Auckland, New Zealand, but that's set to change soon. Next stop, who knows? She loves a good department-store sale, French champagne, shoes and a racy romance novel. And chocolate, naturally.

Books by Sarah Mayberry

HARLEQUIN BLAZE
380—BURNING UP
404—BELOW THE BELT
425—AMOROUS LIAISONS
464—SHE'S GOT IT BAD

HARLEQUIN SUPERROMANCE
1551—A NATURAL FATHER
1599—HOME FOR THE HOLIDAYS

This one is for all my female friends—the passers of tissues, the sharers of chocolate, the givers of hugs. Having a laugh with my mates is one of the small, perfect pleasures in life.

And, as always, no words would be written if it was not for Chris cheering me on from the sidelines and Wanda coaching me from the finish line. You both rock—thank you for your endless patience.

1

WHATEVER YOU DO, don't throw up.

Poppy Birmingham pressed a hand to her stomach. The truth was, if her breakfast was destined to make a reappearance, that hand was hardly going to make a difference. She let her arm drop. She took a deep breath, then another.

A couple of people frowned at her as they pushed through the double doors leading into the *Melbourne Herald*'s busy newsroom. She was acutely aware that they probably recognized her and were, no doubt, wondering what one of Australia's favorite sporting daughters was doing hovering outside a newspaper office, looking as though she was going to either wet her pants or hurl.

Time to go, Birmingham, the coach in her head said. *You signed up for this. Too late to back out now.*

She squared her shoulders and sucked in one last, deep breath. Then she pushed through the double doors. Immediately she was surrounded by noise and low-level excitement. Phones rang, people tapped away at keyboards or talked into phones or across partitions. Printers whirred and photocopiers flashed. In the background, huge windows showcased the city of Melbourne, shiny and new in the morning sunshine after being washed clean by rain overnight.

A few heads raised as she walked the main aisle, follow-

ing the directions she'd been given for the sports department.
She tried to look as though she belonged, as though she'd been
mixing it up with journalists all her life. As though the new
pants suit she was wearing didn't feel alien when she was used
to Lycra, and the smell of stale air and coffee and hot plastic
wasn't strange after years of chlorine and sweat.

The rows of desks seemed to stretch on and on but finally
she spotted Leonard Jenkins's bald head bent over a keyboard
in a coveted corner office. As editor of the sports section on
Melbourne's highest circulating daily newspaper, Leonard
was the guy who assigned stories and had final say on edits
and headlines. He was also the man who'd approached her six
weeks ago and offered her a job as a columnist.

At the time she'd been thrown by the offer. Since she'd
been forced into retirement by a shoulder injury four months
ago she'd been approached to coach other swimmers, to work
with women's groups, to sponsor a charity. A chain of gyms
wanted her to be their spokesperson, someone else wanted her
to endorse their breakfast cereal. Only Leonard's offer opened
the door to new possibilities. For years she'd known nothing
but the black line of the swimming pool and the burn of her
muscles and her lungs. This was a new beginning.

Hence the urge to toss her cookies. She hadn't felt this
nervous since the last time world championships were in
Sydney—when she *had* thrown up spectacularly before her
first heat.

She stopped in front of Leonard's office and was about to
rap on the open door when he lifted his head. In his late fifties,
he was paunchy with heavy bags under his eyes and fingers
stained yellow from nicotine.

"Ah, Poppy. You found us okay. Great to see you," he said
with a smile.

"It's good to be here."

"Why don't I introduce you to the team first up and show you your desk and all that crap," Leonard said. "We've got a department meeting in an hour, so you'll have time to get settled."

"Sounds good," she said, even though her palms were suddenly sweaty. She was hopeless with names. No matter what she did, no matter how hard she tried to concentrate on linking names to faces, they seemed to slip through her mental fingers like soap in the shower.

She wiped her right hand furtively down her trouser leg as Leonard led her to the row of desks immediately outside his office.

"Righteo. This is Johnno, Davo and Hilary," he said. "Racing, golf and basketball."

Which she took to mean were their respective areas of expertise. Johnno was old and pock-faced, Davo was mid-thirties and very tanned, and Hilary was red-haired and in her early thirties, Poppy's age. They all murmured greetings and shook her hand, but she could tell they were keen to get back to their work.

"This mob around here," Leonard said, leading her around the partition, "keep an eye on motor sport. Meet our resident gear heads, Macca and Jonesy."

"All right. Our very own golden girl," Jonesy said. He was in his late twenties and already developing a paunch.

"Bet you get that all the time, huh?" Macca asked. He smiled a little shyly and ran a hand over his thinning blond hair. "Price of winning gold."

"There are worse things to be called," she said with a smile.

Leonard's hand landed in the middle of her back to steer her toward the far corner.

"And last, but not least, our very own Jack Kerouac," he said.

Poppy's palms got sweaty all over again as she saw who he was leading her toward.

Jake Stevens.

Oh, boy.

Her breath got stuck somewhere between her lungs and her mouth as she stared at the back of his dark head.

She didn't need Leonard to tell her that Jake Stevens wrote about football, as well as covering every major sporting event in the world. She'd read his column for years. She'd watched him interview her colleagues but had somehow never crossed paths with him herself. She knew he'd won almost every Australian journalism award at least once. And she'd read his debut novel so many times the spine had cracked on her first copy and she was now onto her second.

He was wonderful—the kind of writer who made it look effortless. The kind of journalist other journalists aspired to be.

Including her, now that she'd joined their ranks.

"Heads up, Jake," Leonard said as they stopped beside the other man's desk.

Not Jakey or some other diminutive, Poppy noted. His desk was bigger, too, taking up twice as much space as those of the other journalists.

Jake Stevens kept them waiting while he finished typing the sentence he was working on. Not long enough to be rude, but enough to make her feel even more self-conscious as she hovered beside Leonard. Finally he swiveled his chair to face them.

"Right. Our new *celebrity columnist,*" he said, stressing the last two words. He looked at her with lazy, deep blue eyes and offered her his hand. "Welcome on board."

She slid her hand into his. She'd only ever seen photographs of him before; he was much better looking in real life. The realization only increased her nervousness.

"It's great to meet you, Mr. Stevens," she said. "I'm a big admirer of your work—I've read your book so many times I can practically recite it."

Jake's dark eyebrows rose. "*Mr. Stevens?* Wow, you must *really* admire me."

The back of her neck prickled with embarrassment. She hadn't meant to sound so stiff and formal. Her embarrassment only increased when his gaze dropped to take in her business-like brown suit and sensibly heeled shoes, finally stopping on her leather satchel. She felt like a schoolgirl having her uniform inspected. She had a sudden sense that he knew exactly how uncomfortable she was in her new clothes and her new shoes and how out of place she felt in her new environment.

"I suppose you must have interviewed Poppy at some time, eh, Jake?" Leonard asked.

"No. Never had the pleasure," Jake said.

He didn't sound very disappointed.

Leonard settled his shoulder against the wall. "Big weekend. Great game between Port and the Swans."

"Yeah. Almost makes you look forward to the finals, doesn't it?" Jake said.

The two men forgot about her for a moment as they talked football. Poppy took the opportunity to study the man who'd written one of her favorite novels.

Every time she read *The Coolabah Tree* she looked at the photograph inside the back cover and wondered about the man behind the cool, slightly cocky smile. He'd been younger when the photo had been taken—twenty-eight or so—but his strong, straight nose, intensely blue eyes and dark hair were essentially unchanged. The seven years that had passed were evident only in the fine lines around his mouth and eyes.

The photo had been a head shot yet for some reason she'd

always imagined he was a big, husky man. He wasn't. Tall, yes, with broad shoulders, but his body was lean and rangy—more a long-distance runner's physique than a footballer's. He was wearing jeans and a wrinkled white shirt, and she found herself staring at his thighs, the long, lean muscles outlined by faded denim.

There was a pause in the conversation and she lifted her gaze to find Jake watching her, a sardonic light in his eyes. For the second time that morning she felt embarrassed heat rush into her face.

"Well, Poppy, that's pretty much everyone," Leonard said, pushing off from the wall. "A few odds and bods on assignment, but you'll meet them later. Your desk is over here."

He headed off. She glanced at Jake one last time before following, ready to say something polite and friendly in parting, but he'd already returned to his work.

Well, okay.

She was frowning as Leonard showed her the desk she'd occupy, wedged into a corner between a potted plant and a pillar. It was obviously a make-do location, slightly separate from the rest of the sports team. Pretty basic—white laminate desk, multiline phone, a computer and a bulletin board fixed to the partition in front of her.

"Have a bit of a look-around in the computer, familiarize yourself with everything," Leonard said, checking his watch. "I'll get Mary, our admin assistant, to fill you in on how to file stories and all that hoopla later. Department meeting's in forty minutes—in the big room near the elevators. Any questions?"

Yes. Is it just my imagination, or is Jake Stevens an arrogant smart-ass?

"No, it all looks good," she said.

It was a relief to be left to her own devices for a few minutes. All those new faces and names, the new environment, the—

Who was she kidding? She was relieved to have a chance to pull herself together because Jake Stevens had rattled her with his mocking eyes and his sarcasm. He'd been one of the reasons she took the job in the first place—the chance to work with him, to learn from the best. Out of all her coworkers, he'd been the least friendly. In fact, he'd been a jerk.

Disappointing.

But not the end of the world. So what if he wasn't the intelligent, funny, insightful man she imagined when she read his book and his articles? She'd probably hardly ever see him. And it wasn't as though she could take his behavior personally. He barely knew her, after all. He was probably a jerk with everyone.

Except he wasn't.

Two hours and one department meeting later, Poppy was forced to face the fact that the charming, witty man she'd imagined Jake to be did exist—for everyone except her.

The first half of the meeting had been a work-in-progress update. Everyone had multiple stories to file after the weekend so there was a lot of discussion and banter amongst her new colleagues. She didn't say anything since she had nothing to contribute, just took notes and listened. Jake was a different person as he mixed it up with the other writers. He laughed, he teased, he good-naturedly accepted ribbing when it came his way. He offered great ideas for other people's stories, made astute comments about what their competitors would be covering. He was like the coolest kid in school—everyone wanted him to notice them, and everyone wanted to sit next to him at the back of the bus.

The second half of the meeting consisted of brainstorming future stories and features. With the Pan-Pacific Swimming

Championship trials coming up, there was a lot of discussion around who would qualify. Naturally, everyone turned to her for her opinion—everyone except Jake, that is.

He didn't so much as glance at her as she discussed the form of the current crop of Australian swimmers, many of whom had been her teammates and competitors until recently.

"Hey, this is like having our own secret weapon," Macca said. "I love that stuff about what happens in the change rooms before a race."

"Yeah. We should definitely do something on that when the finals are closer. Sort of a diary-of-a-swimmer kind of thing," Leonard said. "Really get inside their heads."

"There's plenty of stuff we could cover. Superstitions, lucky charms, that kind of thing," she said.

"Yeah, yeah, great," Leonard said.

Her confidence grew. Maybe this wasn't going to be as daunting as she'd first thought. Sure, she was a fish out of water—literally—but everyone seemed nice and she understood sport and the sporting world and the commitment top athletes had to have to get anywhere. She had something to contribute.

Then she glanced at Jake and saw he was sitting back in his chair, doodling on his pad, clearly bored out of his mind. A small smile curved his mouth, as though he was enjoying a private joke.

It was the same whenever she spoke during the meeting— the same smile, the same doodling as though nothing she had to say could possibly be of any interest.

By the time she returned to her desk, she knew she hadn't imagined his attitude during their introduction. Jake Stevens did not like her. For the life of her, she couldn't understand why. They'd never met before. How could he possibly not like her when he didn't even know her?

She'd barely settled in her chair when her cell phone beeped. She checked it and saw Uncle Charlie had sent her a message:

Good luck. Come out strong and you'll win the race.

She smiled, touched that he'd remembered this was her first day. Of course, Uncle Charlie always remembered the important things.

She composed a return message. She'd bought him a cell phone a year ago so they could stay in touch when she was competing internationally, but he'd never been one hundred percent comfortable with the technology. She could imagine how long it had taken him to key in his short message.

The sound of masculine laughter made her lift her head. Jake was talking with Jonesy at the other man's desk, a cup of coffee in hand. She watched as Jake dropped his head back and laughed loudly.

She returned her attention to the phone, but she could still see him out of the corner of her eye. He said something to Jonesy, slapped the other man on the shoulder, then headed to his own desk. Which meant he was about to walk past hers.

She kept her focus on her phone but was acutely conscious of his approach. When he stopped beside her, her belly tightened. Slowly she lifted her head.

He studied her desk, taking in the heavy reference books she'd brought in with her: a thesaurus, a book on grammar and the Macquarie Dictionary in two neat, chunky volumes. After a short silence, he met her eyes.

"You do know that *A* to *K* comes before *L* to *Z*, right?" he asked. He indicated the dictionaries and she saw she'd inadvertently set them next to each other in the wrong order. He

leaned across and rearranged them, as though she might not
be able to work it out for herself without his help.

"My hot tip for the day," he said, then he moved off, arro-
gance in every line of his body.

She was blushing ferociously. Her third Jake Stevens–
inspired blush for the day. She stared at his back until he
reached his desk, unable to believe he'd taken a swipe at her
so openly. What an asshole.

He thought she was a stupid jock. That was why he'd
been so dismissive when he met her and why he hadn't listened to a word she'd said in the meeting. He thought she
was a dumb hunk of muscle with an instinct for swimming
and nothing to offer on dry land. Certainly nothing to offer
in a newsroom.

She knew his opinion shouldn't matter. It probably
wouldn't, either, if it didn't speak to her deepest fears about
this new direction she'd chosen.

She'd finished high school, but only just. She read a lot,
but she wasn't exactly known for her e-mails and letters. For
the bulk of her life, she'd measured her success in body
lengths and split seconds, not in column inches and words.
Even her parents had been astonished when she accepted this
job. She could still remember the bemused looks her mother
and father had exchanged when she'd told them. Her brother
had laughed outright, thinking she was joking.

She picked up her phone again and stared at her uncle's text:

Come out strong and you'll win the race.

God, how she wished it was as easy as that.

She was filled with a sudden longing for the smell of
chlorine and the humid warmth of the pool. She knew who

she was there, what she was. On dry land, she was still very much a work in progress.

Who cares what he thinks? He doesn't know you, he knows nothing about you. Screw him.

Poppy straightened in her chair. She reached out and deliberately put the *L* to *Z* back where it had been before Jake Stevens gave her his *hot tip for the day.*

She'd beaten some of the toughest athletes in the world. She'd conquered her own nerves and squeezed the ultimate performance from her body. She'd stood on a podium in front of hundreds of thousands of people and held a gold medal high.

One man's opinion didn't mean dick. She was smart, she was resourceful. She could do this job.

JAKE PULLED THE CORK from a bottle of South Australian shiraz and poured himself a glass. He took the bottle with him as he moved from the kitchen into the living room of his South Yarra apartment.

Vintage R.E.M. blasted from his stereo as he dropped onto the couch. His thoughts drifted over the day as he stared out the bay window to the river below. He frowned.

Poppy Birmingham.

He still couldn't believe the stupid pride on Leonard's face as he'd introduced her. As if she was his own private dancing bear. As if he expected Jake to break into applause because a woman who had never put pen to paper in her life had scored the kind of job it took dedicated journalists years to achieve.

He made a rude noise as he thought about the brand-new reference books she'd lined up on her desk. Not a wrinkle on the spine of any of them. What a joke.

He took another mouthful of wine as his gaze drifted to his own desk, tucked into the corner near the window.

He should really fire up his computer and try to get some words down.

He smiled a little grimly. Who was he kidding? He wasn't going to do any writing tonight, just as he hadn't done any real writing for the past few years. It wasn't as though his publisher was breathing down his neck, after all. They'd stopped doing that about five years ago, two years after his first novel had made the bestseller lists, won literary prizes and turned him into a wunderkind of the Australian literary scene.

He'd missed so many deadlines since then, they'd stopped hassling him. Now the only time he was asked when his next book was due out was when he met people for the first time— mostly because they assumed he'd written second, third, fourth books that they simply hadn't heard about. After all, what writer with any ambition to be a novelist wrote only one book and never completed another?

Ladies and gentlemen, I give you Jake Stevens.

He offered a mock bow to his apartment and poured himself another glass of wine.

Like a needle in the groove of a record, his thoughts circled to Poppy Birmingham. He'd never interviewed her, but he'd interviewed plenty like her. He knew without asking that she'd discovered a love of swimming at an early age, been talent scouted by someone-or-other, then spent the next twenty years churning up various pools.

She'd sacrificed school, boyfriends, family, whatever, to be the best. She was disciplined. She was driven. Yada yada. She could probably crack walnuts with her superbly toned thighs and outrun, outswim and out-anything-else him that she chose to do.

She was a professional athlete—and she had no place on a newspaper. Call him old-fashioned, but that was how he felt.

He leaned back on the couch, legs straight in front of him,

feet crossed at the ankle. His stereo stacker switched from REM to U2—the good angry old stuff, not the new soft and happy pop they'd been serving up the last decade.

He swirled the wine around in his glass, shaking his head as he remembered Poppy's brown suit and how wrong she'd looked in it—like a kid playing dress up. No. Like a transvestite, a man shoehorning himself into women's clothing.

Honesty immediately forced him to retract the thought. He might not approve of her hiring, but there was nothing remotely masculine about Poppy. She was tall, true, with swimmer's shoulders. But she was a woman, no doubt about it. The breasts and hips curving her suit had been a dead giveaway there. And she had a woman's face—small nose, big gray eyes, cheekbones. Her mouth was a trifle on the large size for true beauty, but her full lips more than made up for that. And even though she kept her blond hair cropped short, she didn't look even remotely butch.

He took another mouthful of wine. Just because his new "colleague" was easy on the eyes didn't make what Leonard had done any more acceptable. A smile curved his mouth as a thought occurred—if Poppy was anywhere near as inexperienced a writer as he imagined, Leonard was going to have his hands full knocking her columns into shape. It felt like a fitting punishment for a bad decision.

JAKE WALKED TO WORK the next morning, following the bike path that ran alongside the Yarra River all the way into the city. A rowing team sculled past. He watched his breath mist in the air and kept his thoughts on the interview he wanted to score today and not the words he hadn't written last night.

He was the first one in, as usual. He shrugged out of his

coat, hung it and his scarf across the back of his chair then headed for the kitchen to fire up the coffee machine.

Someone had beaten him to it. Poppy Birmingham stood at the counter, spooning sugar into a mug. He counted four teaspoons before she began to stir. That was some sweet tooth.

She glanced over her shoulder as he reached for the coffee carafe, obviously having heard him approach.

"Good—" Her mouth pressed into a thin line when she saw it was him and the rest of her greeting went unsaid. Her dark gray eyes gave him a dismissive once-over. Then she turned back to her sickly sweet coffee.

She was pissed with him because of his gibe about the dictionary yesterday. Probably couldn't conceive of a world where athletic ability didn't open every door. Because he was a contrary bastard, he couldn't resist giving her another prod.

"Bad for you, you know," he said.

She glanced at him and he gestured toward her coffee.

"All that sugar. Bad for you."

"Maybe. But I'll take sweet over bitter any day," she said. She picked up her mug and exited.

He cocked his head to one side. Not a bad comeback— for a jock.

He picked up his own mug and followed her. He couldn't help noting the firm bounce of her ass as she walked. Probably she could crack walnuts with that, too. He wondered idly what she looked like naked. Most swimmers didn't have a lot happening up top, but she clearly had a great ass and great legs.

She sat at her desk. He glanced over her shoulder as he passed. She'd started writing her debut article already. He read the opening line and mentally corrected two grammatical errors. As he'd suspected last night, Leonard was going to have his work cut out for him editing her work into something publishable. Thank God it wasn't Jake's problem.

Then Leonard stopped by his desk midmorning and changed all that.

"No way," Jake said the moment he heard what his boss wanted. "I'm not babysitting the mermaid."

Leonard frowned. "It's not babysitting, it's mentoring. She needs a guiding hand on the tiller for a few weeks while she finds her feet, and you're our best writer."

Jake rubbed his forehead. "Thanks for the compliment. The answer is still no."

"Why not?" Leonard asked bluntly.

Jake looked at the other man assessingly. Then he shrugged. What the hell. What was the worst thing that could happen if he told his boss how he really felt?

"Because Poppy Birmingham doesn't deserve to be here," he said.

He wasn't sure what it was—his raising his voice, a freak flat spot in the background noise, some weird accident of office acoustics—but his words carried a long way. Davo and Macca looked over from where they were talking near the photocopier, Hilary smirked and Mary looked shocked.

At her desk, Poppy's head came up. She swiveled and looked him dead in the eye. For a long moment it felt as though the world held its breath. Then she stood and started walking toward him.

For the first time he understood why the press had once dubbed her the Aussie Amazon—she looked pretty damn impressive striding toward him with a martial light in her eye.

He crossed his arms over his chest and settled back in his chair.

Bring it on. He'd never been afraid of a bit of truth telling.

2

POPPY HAD PROMISED HERSELF she'd speak up if he did something provocative again. She figured broadcasting his antipathy to all and sundry more than qualified.

Leonard looked as though he'd swallowed a frog. Jake simply watched her, his arms crossed over his chest, his expression unreadable.

She offered Leonard a tight smile. "Would you mind if I had a private word with Mr. Stevens?"

Her new boss eyed her uncertainly. His gaze slid to Jake then to her. She widened her smile.

"I promise not to leave any bruises," she said.

Leonard shrugged. "What the hey? Tear him a new one. Save me doing it."

He headed to his office and Poppy turned to face Jake. His mouth was quirked into the irritating almost smile that he'd worn every time she spoke during their meeting yesterday. She wanted to slap it off his face. She couldn't believe that she'd once thought he was good-looking.

"What's your problem?" she asked.

"I don't have a problem."

"Bullshit. You've been taking shots at me since I arrived. I want to know why."

He looked bored. "Sure you do."

"What's that supposed to mean?"

"You don't want to hear what I really think. You want me to be awed by your career and treat you like the department mascot like everyone else," he said.

She sucked in a breath, stung. "That's the last thing I want."

"Well, baby, you sure took the wrong job." He turned away from her, his hands returning to his keyboard. Clearly he thought their conversation was over.

"I'm still waiting to hear what you really think," she said. She crossed her arms over her chest. She figured that way he might not notice how much she was shaking. She didn't think she'd ever been more angry in her life.

He swiveled to face her. "Let me put it this way—how would you feel if your ex-coach suddenly announced I'd be leading the swim team into the next world championships because he liked a couple of articles I'd written?"

"You think I got this job under false pretenses."

"Got a journalism degree?" he asked.

"No."

"Done an internship?"

"You know I haven't."

"Then, yes, I think you didn't earn this job."

She blinked. He spread his hands wide.

"You asked," he said.

"Actually, you offered—to the whole office."

"If you think some of them haven't thought the same thing…" He shrugged.

She glanced at the other journalists who were all eavesdropping shamelessly. Was it possible some of them shared Jake's opinion?

"Leonard came knocking on my door, not the other way around." She sounded defensive, but she couldn't help it.

"You accepted the offer," he said. "You could have said no."

"So I'm not allowed to have a career outside of swimming?" she asked.

"Sure you are. You're even allowed to have this career, since we all know the Australian public is so in love with its sporting heroes they'll probably eat up anything you write with a spoon, even if you can't string two words together. Just don't expect me to like it," he said. "I worked long hours on tin-pot newspapers across the country to get where I am. So has everyone else on this team. I'm not going to give Leonard a standing ovation for valuing my skills so lightly he's slotted a high school graduate into a leading commentator's role just because she looks good in Lycra and happens to swim a mean hundred-meter freestyle. Never going to happen."

Poppy stared at him. He stared back, no longer bored or cool.

"You might have come to this job by working your way through the ranks, but I've earned my chance, too." She hated that her voice quavered, but she wasn't about to retreat. "I'm not going to apologize for the fact that I have a public profile. I've represented this country. I've swum knowing that I'm holding other people's dreams in my hands, not just my own. You don't know what that's like, the kind of pressure that comes with it. And while you're on your high horse judging me, you might want to think about the fact that you wouldn't even have a job if it wasn't for people like me sweating it out every day, daring to dream and daring to try to make those dreams a reality. You'd just be a commentator with nothing to say."

She turned her back on him and walked away.

The other journalists were suddenly very busy, tapping away at their keyboards or shuffling through their papers. She sat at her desk and stared hard at her computer screen, hoping it looked as though she was reading, when in fact, she was trying very, very hard not to cry.

Not because she was upset but because she was *furious*. Her tear ducts always wanted to get involved when she got angry, but she would rather staple something to her forehead than give Jake the Snake the satisfaction of seeing her cry.

Ten minutes later, Macca approached.

"I was just in, speaking to Leonard. I'm going to work with you on your first few articles, until you find your feet," he said.

She stared at him, chin high. "What did he bribe you with?"

"Actually, I volunteered."

She blinked.

"What can I say? I've always had a thing for water sports."

She gave him a doubtful look.

"And I think Jake was out of line," he added. "So what if you haven't earned your stripes in the trenches? Welcome to the real world, pal. People get lucky breaks all the time for a bunch of different reasons. And even if he disagrees with Leonard's decision, being an asshole to you is not the way to deal with it."

"Hear, hear," she said under her breath.

He smiled at her. "So, we cool? You want to show me what you've got so far?"

"Thank you." She was more grateful for his offer—and support—than she cared to admit.

He pulled up a chair beside her. She shifted the computer screen so he could read her article more easily and sat in tense, twitchy silence while he did so. She'd spent a lot of time working on it—all of last night and most of this morning. She knew it wasn't great, but she hoped it was passable.

"Hey, this is pretty good," he said.

She tried not to show how much his opinion meant to her.

She'd already been nervous enough before The Snake had aired his feelings. Now she knew all eyes would be on her maiden effort.

"You can be honest. I'd rather know what's wrong so I can fix it than have you worry about my feelings," she said.

"Relax. Ask anyone, I'm a hard bastard. Open beer bottles with my teeth and everything," Macca said. "If this was utter crap, I'd tell you. I think we can work on a few things, make some of the language less formal and stiff, but otherwise there's not much that needs doing."

Poppy sank back in her seat and let her breath out slowly.

"And if you're free for lunch, I'll give you the lowdown on the office politics," Macca said.

She smiled. Maybe there was an upside to being savaged by an arrogant, know-it-all smart-ass after all—she'd just made her first new friend at the *Herald*.

THAT NIGHT POPPY HAD her second Factual Writing for the Media class at night school. She'd enrolled when Leonard had offered her the job. So far, she'd learned enough to know she had a lot to learn. But that was why she was there, after all.

There was a message from Uncle Charlie when she finally got home. She phoned him on his cell, knowing he'd be up till all hours since he was a notorious insomniac.

"Hey there, Poppy darlin'," he said when he picked up the phone. "I've been waiting for you to call and fill me in on your first day at work."

"Sorry. To be honest, it was a little sucky, and day two was both worse and better. I was kind of holding off on calling until I had something nice to report."

She filled him in on Jake and their argument and the way Macca had come to her aid.

"Bet this Jake idiot didn't know who he was taking on when he took on you," Uncle Charlie said.

She laughed ruefully. "I don't know. I don't think he was exactly cowed by my eloquence. It makes swimming look pretty tame, doesn't it, even with all the egos and rivalries?" she said a little wistfully.

"Missing it, Poppy girl?"

She swung her feet up onto the arm of her couch.

"I miss knowing what I'm good at," she said quietly, thinking over her day at work and how lost she'd felt in class tonight.

"You're good at lots of things."

"Oh, I know—eating, sleeping…"

"You forgot showering and breathing."

They both laughed.

"Just remember you're a champion." He was suddenly very serious. "The best of the best. Don't let some jumped-up pen pusher bring you down. You can do anything you put your mind to."

Uncle Charlie was her biggest fan, her greatest supporter, the only member of her family who'd watched every one of her races, cheered her wins and commiserated her losses.

"You still haven't told me what you want for your birthday," she said.

He turned seventy in a few weeks' time. She already had his present, but asking him what he wanted had become a bit of a ritual for the two of them.

"A pocketful of stardust," he said. "And one of them fancy new left-handed hammers."

She smiled. He had a different answer every time, the old bugger.

"Careful what you wish for."

"Just seeing you will make my day."

She couldn't wait to see his face when she gave him her present. She'd had her first gold medal mounted in a frame alongside a photograph of the two of them at the pool when she was six years old. It was her favorite shot of the two of them. He was in the water beside her, his face attentive and gentle as he guided her arms. She was looking up at him, laughing, trusting him to show her how to get it right.

He always had, too. He'd never let her down, not once.

"Love you, Uncle Charlie," she said.

"Poppy girl, don't go getting all sentimental on me. Nothing more pitiful than an old man sooking into the phone," he said gruffly.

They talked a little longer before she ended the call. She lay on the couch for a few minutes afterward, reviewing the day again.

She was proud of herself for standing her ground against Jake Stevens, but she wished she hadn't had to. The only place she'd ever been aggressive was in the pool. She couldn't remember the last time she'd had a stand-up argument with someone.

Just goes to show, you've led a sheltered life.

She stood and walked to her bedroom. She was pulling her shirt off when she caught sight of a familiar orange book cover on the bookcase beside her bed. The name Jake Stevens spanned the spine in thick black print.

"Uh-uh, not in my bedroom, buddy," she said. She picked up *The Coolabah Tree* with her thumb and forefinger and marched to the kitchen. She dumped the book in the trash can and brushed her hands together theatrically.

"Ha!"

She'd barely gone three paces before her conscience made her swing around. Before she'd met Jake, *The Coolabah Tree* had been one of her favorite books. His being a jerk didn't change any of that.

She fished out the book and walked into her living room. She looked around. Where to put it so it wouldn't bug the hell out of her?

She laughed loudly as an idea hit her. She crossed to the bathroom and put the book amongst the spare toilet-paper rolls she stored in a basket in the corner near her loo.

She was still smiling when she climbed into bed.

"ANYONE WANT A COFFEE?" Poppy asked.

Jake didn't bother looking up from his laptop. There was no way she would bring him a coffee, even if he was stupid enough to ask for one. The three weeks she'd been at the *Herald* hadn't changed a thing between them.

"I'm cool," Davo said.

"White for me," Hilary said.

Jake glanced over his shoulder as Poppy moved to the back of the press box. The room was buzzing with conversation and suppressed excitement. In ten minutes, the Brisbane Lions and the Hawthorn Hawks would duke it out for the Australian Football League Premiership.

Jake still couldn't believe that Leonard had assigned the newest, greenest writer on the staff to cover the AFL Grand Final. It was the biggest event in the Australian sporting calendar, bar none. Even The Melbourne Cup didn't come close. The *Herald* would dedicate over six pages to the game tomorrow—and Poppy hadn't even clocked a month with the paper and had only a handful of columns under her belt.

Granted, her articles had been a pleasant surprise. Warm, funny, smart. She needed to loosen up a little, relax into the role. Stop trying so hard. But in general the stories hadn't been

the disaster he'd been anticipating. Which still didn't make
her qualified to be here.

They'd flown into Brisbane two days ago to cover the
teams' last training sessions and interview players before the
big event, and he'd been keeping an eye on her. What he'd
seen confirmed she was a rookie in every sense of the word.
She interviewed players from a list of questions she'd prepared earlier, reading them off the page. She studiously wrote
down every word they said. She was earnest, eager, diligent—
and way out of her depth. Yesterday, Coach Dickens had
brushed her off when she tried to ask him about an injured
player. She'd been unable to hide her surprise and hurt at the
man's rude rebuff.

Better toughen up, baby, Jake thought as he watched her
wait patiently in the catering line for her chance at the coffee
urn. Most journalists would eat their own young for a good
story. As for common courtesies such as waiting in line…

As if to demonstrate his point, Michael Hague from the *Age*
sauntered up to the line and slipped in ahead of her, chatting
to a colleague already there as though the guy had been saving
him a place. Poppy frowned but didn't say anything.

Jake shook his head. She was too nice. Too squeaky clean
from all that swimming and wholesome food and exercise.
Even if she developed the goods writingwise, she simply didn't
have the killer instinct a journalist required to get the job done.

He was turning to his computer when she stepped out of
line. Hague had just finished filling a cup with coffee and
Poppy reached out and calmly took it from his hand. She
flashed him a big smile and said something. Jake couldn't hear
what it was, but he guessed she was thanking him for helping
her out. Then she calmly filled a second cup for Hilary.

Jake laughed. He couldn't help it. The look on Hague's

face was priceless. Poppy made her way to their corner, her hard-won coffees in hand. Her gaze found his across the crowded box and he grinned at her and she smiled. Then the light in her eyes died and her mouth thinned into a straight, tight line.

Right. For a second there he'd almost forgotten.

He faced his computer.

He was on her shit list. Which was only fair, since she'd been on his ever since he'd learned about her appointment.

He shook the moment off and focused his attention on the field. The Lions and the Hawks had run through their banners and were lined up at the center of the ground. The Australian anthem began to play, the forty-thousand-strong crowd taking up the tune. The buzz of conversation in the press box didn't falter, journalists in general being a pack of unpatriotic heathens. On a hunch Jake glanced over his shoulder. As he'd suspected, Poppy's gaze was fixed on the field and her lips were moving subtly as she mouthed the words to the anthem.

It struck him that of all the journalists here, she was the only one who could even come close to understanding how the thirty-six players below were feeling right now. He had a sudden urge to lean across and ask her, to try and capture the immediate honesty of the moment.

He didn't. Even if she deigned to answer him, just asking the question indicated that he was softening his stance regarding her appointment. Which he wasn't.

The song finished and the crowd roared its excited approval as the two teams began to spread out across the field. Jake tensed, adrenaline quickening his blood. He loved the tribalism of football, the feats of reckless courage, the passion in the stands. It was impossible to watch and not be affected by it. Even after hundreds of kickoffs over many years, he still got excited at each and every game. The day he didn't was the day he would retire, absolutely.

The starting siren echoed and the umpire held the ball high and then bounced it hard into the center of the field. The ruckmen from both teams soared into the air, striving for possession of the ball.

Jake leaned forward, all his attention on the game. Behind him he heard the tap-tap of fingers on a keyboard. He didn't need to look to know it was Poppy. What in hell she had to write about after just ten seconds of play, he had no idea. Forcing his awareness of her out of his mind, he concentrated on the game.

POPPY CHECKED HER WATCH as she stepped into the hotel elevator and punched the button for her floor. By now, most of the players would be drunk or well on their way to it, and probably half of the press corps, too. She'd been too tired to take Macca up on his invitation to join him, Hilary and Jake for a postcoverage drink. Even if she hadn't been hours away from being ready to file her story by the time the others were packing up to go, she'd had enough of The Snake over the past few days to last a lifetime. She wasn't about to subject herself to his irritating presence over a meal. Not for love or money.

She scrubbed her face with her hands as the floor indicator climbed higher. She was officially exhausted. The lead-up to the game, the game itself, the challenging atmosphere of the press box, the awareness that she was part of a team and she needed to deliver—all of it had taken its toll on her over the past couple of days and she felt as though she'd staggered over the finish line of a marathon.

She was painfully aware that she'd been the last of the team to file her stories every day so far. She'd sweated over her introductions, agonized over what quotes to use, fretted over her sign-offs. Writing didn't come naturally to her, and she was beginning to suspect it was something she would always have to work at. No wonder her shoulders felt as though they were carved from marble at the end of each day.

She toed off her shoes as she entered her hotel room. She'd given up on high heels after the first week in her new job. Not only did they make her taller than most men, she couldn't walk in them worth a damn and they made her feet ache. She shed her navy tailored trousers and matching jacket, then her white shirt. Her underwear followed and she made her way to the bathroom and started the shower up. She felt ten different kinds of greasy after a day of being jostled by pushy journalists and fervent football fans and hovering over her laptop, sweating over every word and punctuation mark. She tested the water with her hand and rolled her eyes when it was still cold. Stupid hotel. No one had warned her that the *Herald* were a pack of tightwads when it came to travel expenses. It was like being on the national swim team again.

She glanced at her reflection while she waited for the water to warm. As always, the sight of her new, improved bustline made her frown. She'd never had boobs. Years of training had keep her lean and flat. But now that she'd stopped the weights and the strenuous training sessions and relaxed her strict diet, nature had reasserted itself with a vengeance over the past few months.

She slid her hands onto her breasts, feeling their smooth roundness, lifting them a little, studying the effect in the mirror. She shook her head and let her hands drop to her sides. It was too weird. She wasn't used to them. Kept brushing against things and people. And she'd had to throw out half her wardrobe. Then there was the attention from men. She didn't think she'd ever get used to that. Never in her life had she had so many conversations without eye contact. She'd quickly learned not to take her jacket off if she wanted to be taken seriously. Which meant she wore it pretty much all the time.

The water was warm at last and she stepped beneath the spray. Ten minutes later, she toweled herself off and went in search of food. The room service menu was uninspired. What she really felt like eating was chocolate chip ice cream and a packet of salty, crunchy potato chips. She eyed the minibar for a few seconds, but couldn't bring herself to pay five times the price for something that was readily available in the convenience store two doors down from the hotel.

She pulled on sweatpants and a tank top, decided against a bra since she was making just a quick pig-out run, then zipped up her old swim team sweat top. Her feet in flip-flops, she headed downstairs.

The latest James Bond movie was showing on the hotel's in-house movie service. She smiled to herself as she thought about Daniel Craig in his swim trunks. Sugar, salt and a buff man—not a bad night in.

She was still smiling contentedly when she returned to the hotel five minutes later, loaded down with snack food. She was in the elevator, the doors about to close, when Jake Stevens thrust his arm between them. She stood a little straighter as he stepped inside the car.

Damn it. Was it too much to ask for a few moments' reprieve from his knowing, sarcastic eyes and smug smile?

She moved closer to the corner so there wasn't even the remote chance of brushing shoulders with him.

His gaze flicked over her briefly. Suddenly she was very aware of her wet hair and the fact that she wasn't wearing a bra. She shifted uncomfortably and his gaze dropped to her carrier bag of goodies.

"Having a big night, I see," he said.

"Something like that."

He leaned closer. She fought the need to pull away as he hooked a finger into the top of the bag and peered inside.

"Chocolate-chip ice cream and nacho-cheese corn chips. Interesting combo."

Up close, his eyes were so blue and clear she felt as though she could see all the way through to his soul.

If he had one.

"Do you mind?" she said, jerking the bag away from him.

He raised his eyebrows. She raised hers and gave him a challenging look.

"Just trying to be friendly," he said.

"No, you weren't. You were being a smart-ass, at my expense, as usual. So don't expect me to lie down and take it."

His gaze dropped to her chest, then flicked back to her face. She waited for him to say something suitably smart-assy in response, but he didn't. The lift chimed as they hit her floor.

Thank God.

She stepped out into the corridor. He followed. She frowned, thrown. Then she started walking toward her room, keeping a watch out of the corner of her eye. As she'd feared, he was following her.

She stopped abruptly and he almost walked into her as she swung to face him.

"I don't need an escort to my door, if that's what you're doing," she said. "I don't need anything from you, which I know probably sticks in your craw since your ego is so massive and so fragile you can't handle having a rookie on the team."

Jake cocked his head to one side. Then he smiled sweetly

and pulled a key from his pocket. The number 647 dangled from it. Two rooms up from hers.

Right.

She could feel embarrassed heat rising into her face. Why did this man always make her so self-conscious? It wasn't as though she cared what he thought of her.

She started walking again. She had her key in her hand well before her door was in sight. She shoved it into the lock and pushed her door open as quickly as she could. She caught a last glimpse of his smiling face as she shut the door.

Smug bastard.

She grabbed a spoon from the minibar and ripped the top off the ice cream. She needed to keep an eye on her temper around him. And she had to stop letting him get under her skin. That, or she had to somehow develop Zen-like mind-body control so she could stop herself from blushing in front of him.

Large quantities of chocolate-chip ice cream went a long way to calming her. She turned on the TV and opened the corn chips. An hour into the movie, she was blinking and yawning. When the movie cut to a love scene, she decided to call it quits for the night. She liked watching James run and jump and beat people up, but she wasn't so wild about the mandatory sex scenes. She knew other people liked them, even got disappointed when they didn't get enough of them, but she so didn't get it.

She contemplated the issue as she brushed her teeth.

Sex, in her opinion, was one of the most overrated activities under the sun. She figured she was experienced enough to know—she'd had three lovers in her thirty-one years, and none of them had come even close to being as satisfying as George, her battery-operated, intriguingly shaped friend. Disappointing, but true.

Of course, it was possible that she'd had three dud lovers in a row, but she thought it far more likely that sex, like most anti-aging products and lose-weight-now remedies, was not all it was cracked up to be.

But that was only her opinion.

She spat out toothpaste and rinsed her mouth. Then she climbed into bed. Just before she drifted off, she remembered that moment in the hallway again. Next time she came face-to-face with The Snake, she was going to make sure she was the one who came out on top. Definitely.

THE NEXT DAY SHE CAUGHT A CAB to the airport for her flight home and discovered that while she and the bulk of Australia had been focused on the ups and downs, ins and outs of a red leather ball, the baggage handlers union had decided to go on strike.

The mammoth lines of irate and desperate-looking people winding through the terminal were her first clue that something was up. She collared a passing airport official and he filled her in. The strike was expected to run for at least three days. Most flights had been canceled.

"Damn it," she said.

He held up his hands. "Not my fault, lady."

"I know. Sorry. It's just my uncle's birthday is on Wednesday."

She'd planned to drive to her parents' place in Ballarat, about an hour north of Melbourne, for the party. But at this rate it didn't look as though she was even going to be in the same state come Wednesday.

"Lots of weddings and funerals and births, too," the official said with a shrug. "Nobody likes an airline strike."

He moved off and Poppy stared glumly at his back. This

was not the first time she'd been left stranded by an airline. As a swimmer, she'd been at the mercy of more than her fair share of strikes, bad weather and mechanical failures. Once, the swim team had almost missed an important meet in Sydney thanks to an airline strike, but their coach had had the foresight to hire a minibus and had driven them the thousand kilometers overnight.

A lightbulb went on in Poppy's mind. If it was good enough for Coach Wellington, it was good enough for her. She turned in a circle, looking for the signs for the car rental agencies. She spotted the glowing yellow Hertz sign. Then she spotted the lineup in front of it. Well, she could only try.

Fingers crossed, she headed over to join the masses.

JAKE WOKE, FEELING LIKE CRAP. Headache, furry mouth, seedy stomach—standard hangover material. He groaned as he rolled out of bed and blessed his own foresight in ensuring he had an afternoon flight out of Brisbane and not a morning one. He'd played this game before, after all, and he'd known last night would be a big one. And it had been. He'd lost track of which bar he'd wound up in, and who he'd been drinking with. There had definitely been some disappointed Bears players in the mix, drowning their sorrows. And he could distinctly remember someone singing the Hawk's club song at one stage.

Whatever. A fine time was had by all.

Well, not *quite* all. Some people had chosen to forgo the festivities and hole up in their room with chocolate-chip ice cream and nacho-cheese corn chips.

He rinsed his mouth out as the memory of Poppy's uptight little "I don't need an escort" speech filtered into his mind.

He didn't know what it was about her, but he couldn't seem to resist poking her with a stick. Maybe it was the way her chin came up. Or the martial gleam that came into her eyes. Or maybe it was the pink flush that colored her cheeks when he bested her.

He stepped beneath the shower and lifted his face to the spray. Oh, man, but he needed some grease and some salt and some aspirin. Big-time.

Of course, Ms. Birmingham wouldn't be in search of saturated animal fats this morning. She'd had hers last night, in the quiet privacy of her room.

Someone needed to tell her that road trips were a good opportunity to bond with her colleagues. Especially when you were a newcomer to the team.

He shrugged. Not his problem. And she was unlikely to take advice from him, anyway.

He recalled the way she'd looked last night, hair wet, face devoid of makeup. Sans bra, too, if he made any guess. She had more up top than he'd expected. Definitely a generous handful.

He soaped his belly and wondered again what she'd look like naked. She wasn't his type, but he supposed he could understand why Macca followed her with his eyes whenever he thought no one was watching. She was striking. She could almost look Jake in the eye, she was so tall. He bet she liked to be on top, too.

He stared down at his hard-on.

Okay, maybe she *was* his type. But only because it had been a while since he'd gotten naked with anyone. Four…no, five months. That was when he'd decided that his fledgling relationship with Rachel-from-the-gym was too much of a distraction from the book he still hadn't written.

He turned the water to cold. Brutal, but effective—his erection sank without a trace.

He dressed and packed his luggage. Then he checked out.

"We hope you enjoyed your stay with us, Mr. Stevens," the woman on the reservation desk said. "And we hope the strike doesn't inconvenience you too much."

He lifted his head from signing his credit card slip. "Strike? What strike?"

"The baggage handlers' strike. It looks like it'll last three days minimum at this point. We've had a lot of people coming back from the airport to check in again."

Shit. He had ten days vacation starting tomorrow. He had plans to go fishing with an old college buddy. No way was he going to kick his heels in Brisbane when there were rainbow trout going begging.

He grabbed his bags and headed to the taxi stand. He'd been caught out like this before and he knew that even during a strike there were still planes in the air. He might be able to talk his way onto one of them. And there was always the bus, God forbid, or a rental.

The moment he hit the airport he nixed the idea of talking himself onto a flight. Lines spilled out the door and every person and his dog was on a cell, trying to hustle some other way home.

He turned for the rental desks. No lines there. Bonus. Maybe no one else had thought of driving home yet.

He dropped his bags in front of the counter and smiled at the pretty blonde behind the desk.

"Hey, there. I need to rent a car," he said.

She rolled her eyes. "You and the rest of the country. Sorry, sir, as we announced five minutes ago, we're all sold out."

He kept smiling.

"There must be something. A car due back later today? Something that didn't pass inspection?"

"Many of our cars didn't come in when our customers

heard about the strike. We've been pulling cars in from our other branches, but there's no stock left. I'm very sorry, sir."

She didn't sound very sorry. She sounded as though she'd had a long and stressful day and was privately wishing him to hell.

"There must be something," he said.

"Where are you traveling to?"

He waited for her to start tapping away at her keyboard to find him a car, but she didn't.

"Melbourne."

"The only thing I can suggest is that you hook up with someone else who is driving your way. I know that blond woman over there is going to Melbourne. She got our last car—maybe she'll take pity on you."

Jake turned his head to follow the woman's finger. He stared in disbelief at the back of Poppy Birmingham's head.

"Shit."

"Excuse me, sir?"

There was no way Poppy was going to take pity on him. She'd more than likely laugh in his face—if he gave her the opportunity.

"Is there a bus counter around here?" he asked. He hated bus travel with a passion, but desperate times called for desperate measures. There were trout swimming in the Cobungra River with his name on them, and he intended to be there to catch them.

"They're on the west side of the airport. Just follow the crowd."

"Thanks."

He hefted his bags and started walking. He could see Poppy up ahead, talking on her cell phone. If it were anyone else— a complete stranger—he'd throw himself on her mercy in a split second. But Poppy didn't like him. Admittedly, he'd given her plenty of reasons to feel that way, but the fact remained that she was far more likely to drive over him in her rental car than offer him a lift in it.

He walked past her, wondering how she'd react if he snatched the keys from her hand and made a bolt for it. But she was probably pretty fast on her feet. She had those long legs and hadn't been out all night swilling beer and red wine the way he had.

He kept walking. Then he started thinking about sitting on a bus with seventy-odd other angry travelers, sucking in diesel fumes and reliving horror flashbacks from half a dozen high school excursions.

Man.

He stopped in his tracks. He lowered his chin to his chest. He thought about the bus, then he thought about his pride. Then he turned around and walked to where Poppy was finishing her phone call.

He stopped in front of her. She stared at him blankly. Then her gaze dropped to his luggage. A slow smile curved her mouth. He waited for her to say something, but she didn't.

She was going to make him ask.

Shit.

He took a deep breath. "Going my way?"

Her smile broadened. "I'm sorry, but you're going to have to do much better than that."

She crossed her arms over her chest and waited. He stared at her for a long moment.

Then he braced himself for some heavy-duty sucking up.

3

POPPY STILL COULDN'T BELIEVE she'd let Jake into her car. Even if she drove nonstop like a bat out of hell, she'd sentenced herself to twenty-four hours in The Snake's company in a small enclosed space. Had she been on drugs twenty minutes ago?

She slid him a look. His eyes were hidden behind dark sunglasses but he appeared to be staring out the windshield, his expression unreadable. He hadn't shaved and his face was dark with stubble. He hadn't said a word since they argued over who was driving the first leg and which route out of the city to take.

He resented having to kiss her ass, but she didn't regret making him do it. It was nice to have a bit of power for a change, even if it was only temporary.

She focused on the road. If he wanted to play it strong and silent, that was fine with her. She'd had more than enough of his smart mouth over the past three weeks.

"Do you mind if I turn the air-conditioning on?" he asked ten minutes later.

It was an unseasonably warm day for September and she was starting to feel a little sticky herself.

"Sure."

He fiddled with the controls. "Hmph." He sat back in his seat. "It's broken."

"It can't be."

He turned his head toward her. She didn't need to see his eyes to know he was giving her a look.

"Feel free to check for yourself."

She did, flicking the switch on and off several times. He didn't say a word as the seconds ticked by and no cool air emerged from the air vents.

"Fine. It's broken," she said after a few minutes.

"No shit."

She cracked the window on her side to let some fresh air into the car. He did the same on his side. The road noise was loud, the equivalent of being inside a wind tunnel.

Great. Jake the Snake beside me, and a bloody hurricane roaring in my ear. This is going to be the road trip from hell.

After half an hour she couldn't stand the noise any longer. She shut her window. A short while later, so did Jake.

The temperature in the car rose steadily as the sun moved across the sky. Jake shrugged out of his jacket and so did she. By the time they'd been on the road for two hours, her shirt was sticking to her and sweat was running down her rib cage.

Poppy spotted a sign for a rest area and turned into it when it came up on their left.

Jake stirred and she realized he'd been dozing behind his glasses and not simply staring out the windshield ignoring her.

"You ready to swap?" he asked, pushing his sunglasses up onto his forehead and rubbing his eyes.

"Nope," she said. "I'm changing into something cooler."

She got out of the car and unlocked the trunk. Jake got out, too, stretching his arms high over his head and arching his back. His T-shirt rode up, treating her to a flash of flat belly, complete with a dark-haired happy trail that disappeared beneath the waistband of his jeans. She frowned and looked away, concentrating on digging through her bag in search of her sports tank. When she found it, she gave him a pointed look.

"Do you mind?"

He stared at her.

"What?"

"A little privacy, please." She spun her finger in the air to indicate she wanted him to turn his back.

He snorted. "Lady, we're on a state highway, in case you hadn't noticed. Everyone who drives past is going to cop an eyeful unless you hunker down in the backseat."

"I don't care about everyone else. I have to work with you."

She didn't care if he thought she was prudish or stupid—she was not stripping down to her bra in front of him. She absolutely did not want him knowing what she looked like in her underwear. It was way too personal a piece of information for him to have about her. She wasn't exactly sure how he could turn it to his advantage, but that was beside the point.

He sighed heavily and turned his back.

"If I see anything, I promise to poke an eye out," he said.

She unbuttoned her shirt and shrugged out of it. She checked he still had his back turned. He hadn't moved. Her tank top got tangled in her haste to pull it over her head. She twisted it around the right way and tugged it on. She glanced at him again. This time his face was in quarter profile as he gazed over the acres of grassland running alongside the freeway.

Had he sneaked a look? She stared at him suspiciously, but he didn't so much as blink.

"I'm ready," she said.

He turned and his gaze flicked down her body briefly before returning to her face. She was acutely aware that her tank top was small and tight and a far cry from the business shirts and jackets she'd been wearing to work to date.

She slammed the trunk shut and moved to the driver's side door. He met her there, his hand held out expectantly.

"I'll drive," he said.

"No, you won't."

If he'd asked, maybe she would have considered it. But there was no way she was taking orders from him. They'd be serving ice cream in hell before that happened.

"There's no way you're driving all the way to Melbourne," he said.

"I'm not an idiot. When I'm tired, I'll let you know."

His stared at her, his blue eyes dark with frustration. Then he turned on his heel and returned to his side of the car.

She waited till he had his seat belt on before pulling back onto the highway. Immediately he leaned across and turned the radio on. Static hissed and he fooled around with the dials until he found some music.

Johnny Cash's deep voice filled the car. Poppy forced her shoulders to relax. Jake Stevens got on her nerves. She wished he didn't, but he did. As she'd already acknowledged, she needed to get a grip on her temper when he was around.

It would also be good if she wasn't quite so aware of him physically. Her gaze kept sliding across to where his long legs were stretched out into the footwell. And she kept remembering that flash of flat male belly. It was highly annoying and disconcerting. She didn't like him. She didn't want to be aware of him.

She slid another surreptitious glance his way and tensed when she caught him looking at her. More specifically, at her breasts.

She glared at him until he lifted his gaze and met hers. He had the gall to shrug a shoulder and give her a cocky little smile.

"Hey, what can I say? I'm only human."

"Subhuman, you mean."

"Staring at a woman's breasts is not a capital offense, last time I checked," he said.

"Maybe I don't want you looking at my breasts. Ever think about that?"

"Don't worry, I won't make a habit of it."

She stiffened. What was he saying? That he didn't like her breasts? That he didn't consider them ogleworthy? She glanced down at herself and frowned.

"What's wrong with them?" she asked.

She could have bitten her tongue off the moment the words were out of her mouth. She could feel the mother of all blushes working its way up her neck.

She kept her eyes front and center as he looked at her.

"Relax," he said. "I didn't mean anything by it. Men check out women all the time. It's basic biology."

"I *am* relaxed," she said through her teeth. "And I didn't think you were about to propose because you checked out my rack. I might not be used to having boobs, but I know that much."

She didn't think it was possible, but her blush intensified. She couldn't believe she'd made such a revealing confession to The Snake.

There was a short silence before he spoke.

"I wondered about that," he said. "All the photos I ever saw, you looked about an A cup."

"You made a note of my *cup size?*" she asked, her voice rising.

"Sure. I'm not blind. So, what, you stopped training and puberty kicked in, is that it?"

He spoke conversationally, as though they were talking about the weather. As though it was perfectly natural for him to go around guessing women's breast size. And maybe it was—but not *hers*. She didn't want him looking at her and thinking about her like that. It made her feel distinctly...edgy.

She clenched her hands on the wheel. "We are not talking about my breasts."

"You brought it up."

"I did not! You were staring at me!"

"Because you changed into that teeny, tiny tank. I could hardly pretend I didn't notice."

"The air-conditioning is broken and I was hot and you could have tried. A gentleman would have," she said.

He laughed. "A gentleman? Baby, I'm a journalist. I wouldn't have a job if I was a gentleman. Something you better learn pretty quick if you want to survive in this game."

She held up a hand. "Spare me your sage advice, Yoda. You're about three weeks too late to apply for the position of mentor."

He shrugged. "Suit yourself."

"I will, thank you."

"Always have to have the last word, don't you?"

"Look who's talking."

"Thank you for proving my point."

She pressed her lips together, even though she was aching to fire back at him.

He angled his seat back and stretched out, his arms crooked behind his head. "Do you miss it?"

"I beg your pardon?"

"Swimming. Training. Being on the team. Do you miss it?"

She made a rude noise in the back of her throat. "Just because we're stuck in a car for a few hours doesn't mean we have to talk."

"It's a long drive."

"I'm not here to entertain you."

He was silent for a moment. She flipped the visor to the side to block the sun as it began its descent into the west.

"Okay, what about this? I get a question, then you get one. Quid pro quo."

"Thank you, Dr. Lecter, but I don't want to play."

"Why? What are you scared of?"

She shifted in her seat. He was goading her, daring her. She knew it was childish, but she didn't want him thinking he could best her so easily.

"Fine," she said. "Yes, I miss swimming. It was my life for twenty-five years. Of course I miss it."

"What do you miss the most?"

"You think I can't count? It's my turn. Why haven't you published a follow-up to *The Coolabah Tree?*"

She could feel him bristle.

"I'm working on one now," he said stiffly.

"What's it called?"

"Nice try. Why do you want to be a journalist?"

"Because it's not swimming. And because I feel I have something to offer. How long did it take you to write your first book?"

"Two years, working weekends and nights."

"How many drafts did you do?"

"Three. And that was two questions."

"You answered them."

He shrugged. "Do you ever think about the four-hundred-meter final at Beijing? Wish you could go back again?"

She should have known he'd bring that up. The lowest point in her swimming career—of course he'd want to stick his finger in the sore spot and see if she squirmed.

She put the indicator on and pulled into the approaching rest stop.

"What's wrong?" he asked.

"I'm tired."

"Right."

She got out and stretched her back. She was aware of Jake doing the same thing on the other side of the car. Dusk was falling and the world around them was muted in the fading light. They crossed in front of the car as they swapped sides.

She waited until he was on the highway again before answering his question.

"I used to think about it all the time, but not so much now. I had my chance and I missed it and I came home with silver instead of gold. I had a bunch of excuses for myself at the time, but the fact is that I simply didn't bring my best game on the day. It happens. If you can't live with your own mistakes, competing for a living will kill you."

"You're very philosophical."

"Like I said, I used to think about it a lot. But you can't live in the past."

He reached up and adjusted the rearview mirror. "Your turn."

She studied his profile. He was a good-looking man. Charming and interesting—when he wanted to be. Not that she'd experienced any of that firsthand, but she had eyes in her head. He'd cut a swath through the female contingent in the press box with his boyish grin and quick wit.

"Why aren't you married?" she asked before she could censor herself.

He frowned at the road. "I was. We divorced five years ago."

"Oh." She hadn't expected that. Watching him at work, the way he came in early and left late, she'd figured him for a loner, one of those men who had dodged commitment so many times it had become a way of life. But he'd been married. And he sounded unhappy that he wasn't still married.

"What about you? Why aren't you married?"

She smiled ruefully. Quid pro quo, indeed. "No one's ever asked me."

He glanced at her, a half smile on his mouth. "That's a cop-out."

She shrugged. "Maybe, but that's all you're going to get."

They lapsed into silence, even though it was her turn to ask a question.

"We should stop for food soon. And start thinking about where we're going to stay the night," he said.

They wound up at McDonald's since it was the only thing on offer. They studied the road map as they ate, deciding on Tamworth as their destination for the evening.

"There'll be a decent motel there, and a few places to eat," Jake said.

She pushed the remains of her burger and fries away.

"You going to eat those?" Jake asked, eyeing her fries.

"Go nuts."

He polished them off then went back to the counter to order an apple pie for the road.

She waited outside in the cold night air, looking up at the dark sky, listening to the rush of cars on the highway and marveling that she and Jake Stevens had spent several hours in a car together and no blood had been spilled.

Yet.

"Okay, let's hit the road," he said as he joined her in the parking lot.

She glanced at him, straight into his blue eyes. They stared at each other a moment too long before she turned away. He walked ahead of her as they crossed to the car. She found herself staring at his butt. She'd always had a thing for backsides and he had a nice one. Okay—a *very* nice one.

Why am I noticing Jake the Snake's butt?

She frowned and looked away. Must be the car equivalent of Stockholm Syndrome. At least she hoped that was what it was.

POPPY WAS DRIVING AGAIN when they pulled into Tamworth just before eight o'clock. Apart from one small disagreement over radio stations, their unofficial cease-fire was still in effect. Jake craned his head to read the brightly illuminated signs of the various motels as they cruised Tamworth's busy main street.

"That place, over there," he said, pointing to a blue-and-white neon sign in front of a brown-brick, two-story motel. "They've got spa baths."

She rolled her eyes but pulled over, since she didn't have a better suggestion.

"Park the car and I'll get us some rooms," he said.

Before she could say anything, he was out of the car and striding toward reception.

"Yes, sir," she said to herself. "Three bags full, sir. Have you any wool, sir?"

Because it would rankle too much to obey him to the letter, she joined him in reception as he was handing over his credit card to the middle-aged clerk.

"Hang on a minute," she said. "I'll pay for my own room."

"You got the car. I'll get this."

It was a perfectly reasonable argument but she opened her mouth to dispute it anyway.

"We can argue after dinner," he said. "You can arm wrestle me to the floor and pound me into submission."

"What makes you think I'm having dinner with you?"

"Because you can't sit in your room and eat ice cream and chips two nights in a row. You'll get scurvy. You need vitamin C."

The desk clerk was watching their interplay curiously. Poppy took her room key.

"This doesn't mean I'm having dinner with you," she said.

But after she'd had a long shower and changed into fresh clothes, the sterile cleanliness of the room started to get to her. Plus she was hungry. When Jake knocked on her door ten minutes later, she pocketed her room key and stepped outside.

"There's a steak place up the road," he said.

He hadn't doubted her for a moment, the smug bastard.

"This is only because I'm hungry and they don't have room service," she said.

"It's all right. I didn't think you were about to propose because you agreed to have dinner with me."

He was deliberately echoing her words from during their ill-fated breast discussion. She couldn't help it—she cracked a smile.

"You are such a smart-ass," she said.

"You're no slouch yourself."

"No, I'm strictly amateur hour compared to you. You're world-class."

They started walking toward the glowing roadside sign for Lou's Steakhouse.

"Now you've made me nervous," he said.

"Sure I have."

"You have. World-class—that's a lot to live up to. You've given me performance anxiety."

"I bet you've never had performance anxiety in your life."

"That was before I met you."

She became aware that she was still smiling and slowing her steps, dawdling to prolong their short walk to the restaurant. She frowned, suddenly uneasy. She looked at him and saw that he was watching her, an arrested expression on his face. As though, like her, he'd just realized that they were enjoying each other's company.

Good Lord. Next thing you know, the moon will be blue and a pig will fly by.

She lengthened her stride and fixed her gaze on the steak house. The sooner this evening—this *drive*—was over, the better.

"YOU ARE SO WRONG. He meant to get busted. Why else would he volunteer to do a second drug test when he'd already been cleared?"

Poppy leaned across the table as she spoke, one elbow propped on the red-and-white tablecloth. Jake tried not to smile at the earnest determination in her expression. She was pretty cute when she got all passionate about something.

They were the only customers left in the restaurant, even though it was barely ten. They'd been talking sports throughout the meal, their current topic being the recent drug scandal involving a well-known British cyclist.

"There's no way anyone would throw away their career like that. He's banned from cycling for life. He's lost his sponsors. He's screwed," he said.

She nodded enthusiastically. "Exactly, and that's what he wanted. Why else would he take that second test?"

The neck of her shirt gaped. Not for the first time that evening he noticed the lacy edge of her bra and wondered if she knew her underwear was on display. He suspected not—Poppy didn't strike him as the kind of woman who seduced with glimpses of lace and skin. She probably had no idea one of her buttons had slipped free.

Maybe it made him an opportunist, but he wasn't about to tell her. Not when the view was so rewarding.

He returned his attention to her face, aware that his jeans were a little snug around the crotch all of a sudden.

"No way. I just don't buy that anyone would throw it all away like that."

"You don't know what it's like," she said darkly. "Everyone looking at you, pinning their hopes on you, channeling all their ambitions and dreams into your life, your career, your achievements. Maybe he self-destructed rather than risk failing on the track."

He studied her. She looked so sunny and uncomplicated, even after several glasses of wine and a long day on the road. He couldn't imagine her ever wanting to throw her career in.

"Is this a confession? Did you injure your shoulder on purpose so you'd miss the World Championships?" he asked lightly.

She reached for her wine and took a big swallow. "You're joking, I know, but there were definitely times when I thought it would be easier if I simply couldn't swim anymore. Not because I decided not to, you know, but because I just *couldn't* and the decision was taken out of my hands."

"And then you got injured."

"Yep, I did. And I discovered that the grass is always greener."

She laughed, then shrugged self-deprecatingly. "It's not like I could keep swimming forever. There are girls coming up now who are so strong and fast…. I would have been a dinosaur wallowing around the pool in a few more years."

She picked up the dessert menu and studied it. He took the opportunity to study her. She looked like everybody's idea of a poster girl for Australian swimming, the kind of athlete you'd find smiling from the back of a cereal box: the blond hair, the clear skin, the frank way she had of meeting his eye whenever she spoke. But she was more complicated than that. She was funny. She was honest. She was smart. She questioned things, was curious about the world.

He liked her.

"How have things been going with Macca?" he asked. "He been helping you out with your columns okay?"

She'd been about to take another mouthful of wine but she froze with the glass halfway to her mouth. She stared at him for a long moment, then put her glass down.

"Dear Lord. Someone pinch me—Jake Stevens has got a conscience."

He shifted in his chair. "I might be a smart-ass, but I'm not an asshole."

She raised an eyebrow. For some reason it seemed very important to him that she not believe the worst of him.

"I owe you an apology." The words came out a little stiffly but he was determined to set things right. "I shouldn't have taken my frustration with Leonard out on you."

"No, you shouldn't have."

"It's not your fault he turned into a publicity whore. And you've done a good job."

She raised a hand to her forehead and blinked rapidly. "Wow. Is there a gas leak in the room or did you just pay me a compliment?"

He poured himself more wine. They were both a little tipsy, which was no bad thing given the turn the conversation had taken.

"Okay, maybe I have been an asshole," he admitted.

"It's okay. You gave me something to worry about other than my writing. And you were entitled to be pissed about the situation—just not at me."

She smiled. He smiled back.

"You're being very generous," he said.

"I think I'm a little drunk. No doubt I'll regret not making you grovel more in the morning."

"That wasn't groveling. That was an apology."

"You say tomato…"

She was laughing at him, her gray eyes alight with humor. He raised his glass.

"To starting again."

She clinked glasses with him.

"To learning from the best," she said.

He frowned, then shook his head ruefully as he took her meaning. "You don't want me mentoring you. I'm a smart-ass, remember?"

"You're right, I don't. But I want your advice sometimes. I want to know when I'm screwing up and haven't realized it yet. You're the best writer on the paper. I'd be an idiot not to learn from you if I can."

She held his eye as she said it. There was no denying he was flattered. And a little embarrassed by her unflinching assessment.

"Macca's pretty good. And Hilary's up for a Walkley Award this year."

"Modesty, Mr. Stevens? I'm surprised." She propped her elbow on the table again and leaned her chin on her hand. "Come on, hit me with your next hot tip for the day. What do I need to know? Where have I gone wrong so far?"

He winced at the reminder of his comment regarding her reference books. Not his kindest act. He owed her.

"You should have come out with us last night," he said. "Everyone's tired after a long haul like the Grand Final, but you missed out on a chance to be part of the team."

She frowned, processing what he'd said.

"Okay, fair enough. Next time, I'll come out to play. What else?"

He poured her more wine and topped up his own glass. The waitstaff were standing at the counter looking bored, but he figured if they wanted Poppy and him to leave they could say so.

"You need to be tougher. When Coach Dickens ignored you the other day when you asked for a comment, you backed off. You should have tried again, said something to get his attention, made him stop and engage with you."

"I didn't want to alienate him. I know what it's like when the press get in your face."

"That's our job. He gets paid a lot of money to do what he does. If he didn't want the fame and glory, he'd be at home watching it on TV like everyone else."

She nodded. "I'll try to be pushier. Even if it does make my toes curl."

He settled back in his chair and let his gaze dip below her face again. He'd been thinking about her breasts on and off ever since their conversation in the car. He wondered if they were as firm as they looked. And if her skin was as warm and smooth as he imagined.

"One thing you should think about," he said. "The players. Football, tennis, cricket, it doesn't matter—they're hound dogs, even a lot of the married ones. No matter what, don't go there. Shortest route to trashing your career."

She waved a hand dismissively. "Not a problem. Next."

"I'm serious. Remember Joanne Hendricks? She would have been in line for Leonard's job by now if she was still around."

He didn't need to say more. He could see from Poppy's expression that she remembered the furor that had erupted when the high-profile journalist's affair with a married rugby player had gone public. She'd subsequently been forced to resign from the *Herald*.

"I take your point, but it's not an issue."

"You say that now, but I've seen some of those guys go to

work on a woman. They can be bloody charming when they want something."

Poppy made a frustrated sound. "As if I'm going to jeopardize my career for a bunch of pointless fumbling and huffing and puffing. I'm not a *man*." She drained her wineglass.

"*Huffing and puffing?* And what does being a man have to do with it?"

"Sex is for men," she said simply. "You get off on it more, therefore you're more likely to be idiots about it."

She said it as though reporting proven medical fact. He raised his eyebrows and leaned toward her.

"Let me get this straight—women don't enjoy sex? Is that your contention?"

"I can't speak for all women. But I bet I'm not the only one who thinks it's overrated."

She was drunk. That was the only reason she would ever say something so personal and revealing to him. If he were a gentleman, he'd ignore it and move on.

"You think sex is overrated?"

"In a word, yes."

"Baby, you're *so* doing something wrong."

She shook her head. "No. I've done it enough to know. Sex is like an Easter egg—big and impressive on the outside, but empty on the inside. All promise, no delivery."

"You've never had an orgasm," he said with absolute certainty.

"On the contrary. I have had many, thanks to the marvels of modern technology. Which is more than I can say for sex."

Oh, man, was she going to regret this conversation in the morning.

"There's no way a piece of plastic and silicone can match the satisfaction of real sex," he said.

"Your opinion. I'd take twenty minutes with George over

twenty minutes with a man any day. He never talks back, he always does what I want and he always delivers at least once."

"George? Your vibrator is called George?"

"After George Clooney."

He shook his head.

"You can't handle it because male egos like to think that women get off as much as they do during sex. It's a prowess thing."

"I don't *think* anything. I *know* women have a good time in bed with me."

She shook her head slowly.

"Remember the diner scene from *When Harry Met Sally?*" She thumped her fists on the table a couple of times. "Oh, yes. *Yesss. Yesss!*" She slumped in her chair languorously, ran a hand through her hair and looked at him with heavy, smoky eyes.

He had to admit, it was a pretty damn convincing impersonation of a woman having an orgasm.

She sat up straight and smiled at him. "I rest my case."

He narrowed his eyes at her. "Why do women have sex then if they don't enjoy it as much?"

"Because they want to keep men happy. Because they want them to put the garbage out and catch spiders and change the oil in the car and they understand sex is the currency of choice when dealing with the male of the species."

Jake simply couldn't believe a woman could be so messed up about something so simple.

"Come on," he said, standing. He threw some money on the table to cover their bill.

"It's not your fault. It's biology. You scored the penis. Every time you put it inside something, it feels good. We scored the clitoris. If they'd really known what they were doing, whoever designed human beings would have put it *inside* the vagina."

She was talking loudly and the staff were exchanging looks. He grabbed her hand and towed her out of the restaurant.

"The clitoris works just fine where it is," he said, leading her back toward the motel.

"With George on the job it does."

She stumbled and he steadied her. She rambled some more about the differences between men's and women's bodies as they completed the short walk to the motel. He was too busy focusing on reaching his room ASAP to pay much attention. Finally he opened his door and led her inside.

She blinked as she looked around. "This isn't my room."

"Nope. It's mine."

He kicked off his shoes. She blinked at that, too.

"What are you doing?"

"Setting you straight." He glanced over his shoulder at the clock on the bedstand. "Does the twenty minutes start from now or when we get naked?"

She stared at him for a long moment.

"You're drunk."

"So are you."

"Not that drunk."

"Me, either. So what are you waiting for?"

She hesitated another beat. Then her gaze dropped to his crotch where he was already hard for her. Her mouth opened. He swore her pupils dilated. Then she started shrugging out of her jacket.

"I hope your ego can handle this," she said.

"I hope your body can handle this," he said.

She pulled her shirt off and he stared at her full, lush breasts, covered in white lace. He was already hard, but he got a whole lot harder.

"Your time starts now," she said.

4

POPPY REACHED BEHIND HERSELF to unclasp her bra. If she stopped to think about it, she knew she'd lose her nerve. This was nuts. Absolutely bonkers.

For starters, until a few hours ago she'd loathed Jake Stevens, and she was pretty sure the feeling had been mutual. Then there was the small fact that she worked with him.

So why was she sliding her straps off her shoulders and letting her bra fall to the carpet?

Jake made a small, satisfied sound as he saw her breasts. Heat swept through her.

That was why—the rush of hot, sticky sensation that had hit her every time she'd caught Jake staring at her breasts over dinner.

He was attracted to her. He wanted to get her naked, touch her breasts, slide inside her.

And even though she was almost certain the buildup would be more fun than the actual main event, she wanted to do all those things, too.

"For the record, in case you have any doubts at all, you have great breasts," Jake said, his gaze intent on her. "Really, really great."

He stripped off his T-shirt and she stared at his broad shoulders and lean belly. He was tall and rangy but still firm and lean with muscle. Dark hair covered his pectoral muscles before trailing south. Her gaze dropped to his thighs where his erection was clearly visible against the denim of his jeans.

She imagined what he would look like—long and thick and hard. Need throbbed between her thighs.

She undid her belt and unzipped her fly, then worked her jeans over her hips. She hesitated, unsure whether to take her panties off at the same time. She shrugged; they were on the clock, after all. Might as well give him a fighting chance. She slid her thumbs into the side elastic of her underwear and tugged them off with her jeans. She kicked the lot to one side and looked at him.

He was pushing his jeans and underwear down his legs and his erection bounced free. Her eyes widened as she saw how big he was, how hard.

Oh, boy.

He looked up from kicking his clothes to one side and grinned when he saw her face. Then his gaze dropped to study her legs, her hips, the neat curls between her thighs.

"Come here," he said, crooking his finger.

She took a small step forward, all her doubts clamoring for attention. This was a bad idea. Really, really bad.

Jake closed the remaining distance between them. She opened her mouth to tell him she'd made a mistake, that she was sober now and this was a crazy. He reached out and slid both hands onto her breasts. His hands were warm and firm, and he locked eyes with her as he cupped her in his palms, then swept a thumb over each nipple. She bit her lip. He squeezed her nipples between his fingers, rolling them gently.

"Nice?" he said, his breath warm on her face.

"Yes."

"Good."

He lowered his head. She closed her eyes as his mouth covered hers, soft yet firm, his tongue sweeping into her mouth. He brought his body against hers, her breasts pressing against his chest, his erection jutting into her belly. His skin felt incredibly hot where it touched hers, his body hard where hers was soft.

He tasted of wine. His tongue teased hers, wet and hot. She shivered as his hand slid across her lower belly.

"Normally, we'd fool around a little more than this before I made a play for third base," he murmured as he kissed his way across to her ear. "But my honor's at stake here. So if you don't mind, I'm going to go for it."

She let her head drop back as he slid his tongue into her ear.

"I think I can make an exception this once," she said.

The truth was, she didn't know if it was the wine or the situation or Jake himself, but she could feel how wet she was for him already. Tension had been building between them all night. His clear blue eyes watching her across the table. The way he'd teased her. The way he'd looked at her body. It had all been leading to this moment. Why else had she issued her challenge?

And it *had* been a challenge. Definitely.

She shivered as he slid a single finger into the folds of her sex. Her hands gripped his shoulders as his finger slicked over her clitoris and then slid farther still until he was at her entrance.

Slowly, he circled his finger. She widened her stance, clenching her muscles in anticipation of his penetration. And then he slid his finger inside her. She tightened around him and he gave an encouraging groan.

"You're very tight, Poppy," he said near her ear.

She gasped as his thumb slid onto her clitoris and began to work her while his single, long finger remained inside her.

His other hand toyed with her breasts, plucking at her nipples, squeezing them, teasing them.

She ran her hands across his back and slid her hands onto his ass. It was every bit as firm and hard as she'd imagined it would be. She squeezed it, imagining holding him just like this as he stroked himself inside her.

Her legs started to tremble. She realized she was panting.

Jake walked her backward a few steps, his thumb still circling her clitoris. She felt the mattress behind her knees and sat willingly, lying backward and spreading her legs as he followed her down.

"Yes," he said as began to work his finger inside her, sliding in and out. She lifted her hips, wanting more. He lowered his head and drew a nipple into his mouth.

Men had touched her breasts before. They'd sucked on her nipples, bitten them. But none of them had made her moan the way Jake did. He alternated between licking and sucking and rasping the flat of his tongue over her, and it drove her crazy. She spread her legs wider, wanting more than just his hand between her thighs.

That was new, too—the need to be full, to have his erection inside her.

"I want you," she panted. "I want you inside me."

"Not yet."

She reached between their bodies to find his cock. It was very hard and she found a single bead of moisture on the head of it as she wrapped her fingers around him.

"Now," she said, stroking her hand up and down his shaft.

"Not yet," he repeated.

He slid another finger inside her and his thumb began to pluck at her clitoris, as well as circle it.

"Ohhh," she moaned, letting her head drop back.

Tension built inside her. She realized with surprise that she was close to coming.

Unbelievable. She gripped his shoulders, her whole body tensing.

He slid his hand from between her thighs. Her eyes snapped open and she saw that he was smiling and looking very pleased with himself.

"Don't you dare stop," she said.

He glanced at the bedside unit.

"There's still seven minutes on the clock. Just wanted to check in. How am I faring compared to George?"

She frowned and reached for his hand, placing it back between her thighs.

"Badly. George never stops before I say so."

He laughed. "You're not nearly ready yet, baby."

Then he lowered his head and licked first one nipple, then the other. Then he began kissing his way down her belly.

"Oh," she said.

She couldn't see his face, but she knew he was smiling again as he settled himself between her widespread thighs. Her hands fisted in the sheets as he opened his mouth and pressed a wet, juicy kiss to her sex. He pulled her clitoris into his mouth and began to trill his tongue against it, the sensation so intense, so erotic she gasped.

"Oh!" she moaned.

He slid a finger inside her, then another. Her whole body was trembling. She held her breath as her climax rose inside her.

And again Jake pulled away.

She opened her eyes and stared at him in disbelief. "You have got to be kidding."

She was ready to kill him—but not before she'd jumped him and taken what he refused to give her.

"Two minutes left on the clock," he said. "I'm a man on a mission."

He reached for his jeans pocket and pulled out a condom. She propped herself up on her elbows and watched as he stroked the latex onto himself. For some reason, it turned her on even more, watching him touch himself so intimately.

He caught her eye as he moved over her. Her breasts flattened against his chest and her hips accepted his weight as she felt the tip of his erection probing her wet entrance.

She tilted her hips greedily, and he obliged her by sliding inside her with one powerful stroke.

She forgot to breathe. He was big. Almost too big. She could feel herself stretch to accommodate him. He flexed his hips and stroked out of her. She clutched at his ass and dragged him back inside.

"That. Feels. Amazing," she said.

"Damn straight." He sounded as surprised as she felt.

He began to pump into her, long, smooth strokes that made her gasp and cry out and circle her hips. And then suddenly, at last, her whole body was shaking and she let out a long, low moan as she came and came and came.

She'd barely floated down to earth before Jake kissed her, his mouth hard on hers. He tensed. His breath came out in a rush. Then he thrust into her one last time and stayed there, his cock buried to the hilt. His body shuddered for long moments, then softened. After a few seconds he opened his eyes and stared down into hers.

"Want me to go get George from your room?" he asked.

He was so smug, so sure of the answer. But she was too blown away to care.

"No." She felt dazed, overwhelmed.

He withdrew from her and rolled away, disappearing into

the bathroom. She pressed a hand between her legs. Everything felt hot down there, hot and throbbing and wet. And supremely, hugely satisfied.

Jake's eyebrows rose when he stepped back into the room and saw where she had her hand, but he didn't say anything.

"Just making sure it's all still there," she said.

He smiled. "Want a bath?"

She registered the sound of running water. Right. He'd chosen the motel with the spa baths.

"Okay."

She moved to the edge of the bed and stood. Ridiculously, her legs faltered as she took her first step, as though her knees had forgotten how to do their thing. Jake's smile widened into a grin.

"Wow. I've never crippled a woman before."

"It could have been a fluke, you know. A one-off. A freak occurrence, never to be repeated."

He stepped close and slid a hand between her thighs where she was still tender and throbbing from his ministrations. He kept his fingers flat, exerting the faintest of pressures on her sensitized flesh.

"You should probably know that I do my best work over long distances," he said, his voice very low, his eyes holding hers. "So if you're issuing another challenge, you better make sure you're up to it."

Despite the fact that she'd just had an orgasm that rocked her world, a shiver of anticipation tightened her body.

"I'm going to take that as a yes," he said.

She reached for him, sliding her hands over his shoulders, his chest, his flat belly, until finally she found his cock, already growing thick and hard again.

"Bring it on," she said.

SHE WAS INCREDIBLE. Jake wanted to be inside Poppy again, wanted to feel the tight grip of her heat around him. But first he wanted to drive her crazy once more, watch her eyes grow cloudy with need, listen to her pant and gasp and beg for him.

He led her into the bathroom where the tub was already half full. Bubbles foamed on top of the water. She followed him into the tub and he experienced a small moment of regret as her breasts disappeared beneath the foam.

They were way too good to hide. Twin works of art. Silky smooth. So responsive he'd almost lost it just playing with her nipples.

Which begged the question, what the hell had the other guys she'd slept with been doing that she'd had to resort to a battery-operated substitute to get off? She wasn't remotely frigid or unresponsive or prudish. She'd been so wet and hot for it, he simply couldn't understand how she could have gone unsatisfied for so long.

She settled against the edge of the tub, her arms spread along the rim. He sat opposite her, letting his legs tangle with hers beneath the water. She was still flushed, her eyes smoky. His gaze found her nipples as they broke the surface of the water.

"So, these other guys you slept with—were they swimmers?" he asked.

She eyed him warily. "Why? You planning on writing an exposé?"

"Just working on a theory. Were they all swimmers?"

"Yes."

"Ah."

He sank deeper into the water.

"*Ah* what? You can't just say *ah* then not explain."

"I'm not surprised things were tepid in the sack. You

trained together, ate together, hung out together. Kind of like brothers and sisters."

"Nothing like brothers and sisters. Not even close."

"Then maybe it was all the training. Maybe they were so beat from all those laps they didn't have anything extra to give."

She thought for a minute. "Maybe."

"Plus, I'm pretty good in bed," he said, to get a rise out of her. "We should definitely not overlook my awesome technique."

She laughed. "You want a medal? A badge of honor?"

He eyed the rosy peaks of her breasts. "How about an encore? Come here."

She hesitated a moment, the way she had earlier when he'd invited her to step closer. He hooked his foot behind her hip and tried to pull her toward him. "I'll make it worth your while."

Her mouth quirked into a smile. "Yeah? How so?"

"Come here and I'll show you."

She pushed away from the edge of the tub and floated toward him. He slid his arms around her and pulled her close for a kiss.

She had a great mouth. He couldn't get enough of it. He shifted in the water until she was straddling him. He deepened their kiss, his hands roaming over her breasts. She tensed slightly every time he plucked her nipples, a shiver of need rippling through her. It drove him wild.

He slid a hand between her thighs to where she was spread wide for him. She was slick and silky beneath his hands. He took his time exploring her, playing with her clitoris, teasing her inner lips, sliding one finger, then two inside her.

"Jake," she whispered, reaching for his cock.

He wanted it, too, but they couldn't use a condom in the water. She seemed to understand as he continued to work her with his fingers. She stroked her hand up and down his length as he stroked his fingers between her thighs. Soon she was shuddering, close to coming again. He was too greedy to let her climax without him.

"Let's go," he said, his voice very low.

She stood and stepped from the spa. She didn't bother toweling herself dry, simply strode straight into the bedroom and reached for his jeans.

"You'd better have another condom," she said.

She smiled triumphantly as she pulled the foil square from his back pocket.

"That's it, though," he said.

"Then we'd better make it count."

She climbed onto the bed on all fours, offering him a heart-stopping view of her slick heat and her firm, toned ass. She looked over her shoulder at him, her skin still glistening from the bath.

"What are you waiting for?"

"Excellent question."

He sheathed himself and moved to the bed. She arched her back and pressed into his hips as he came up behind her. He steadied his cock with his hand and slid it along the slick seam of her sex. She sighed and pressed back some more.

"Stop teasing," she said.

"Stop being so impatient."

But he loved how much she wanted it. He especially loved how wet she was. He pressed forward, the head of his penis sliding just inside her entrance. She arched her spine and took all of him. He closed his eyes as she clenched her muscles around him.

So good. So damned good.

He began to move, withdrawing until just the tip of his cock remained inside her then resheathing himself. She rocked to his rhythm, her body very warm and tight around him. Slowly the tension increased. He slid a hand over her hip and between her thighs. Her clit was swollen and slick and he'd barely touched it before she started to shudder around him.

"Yes. Oh, yes!" she panted.

Man, but she was hot. Tight, wet, her body firm and strong. He closed his eyes as his climax hit him, his hands gripping her hips as he pumped into her once, twice, then one last time.

They were both breathing heavily afterward. He withdrew from her and stepped into the bathroom to dispose of the condom. When he returned, she was lying on her side, the same dazed, slightly lost expression on her face she'd had the first time.

"You okay?" he asked.

"I think so. I feel like I just found out the earth is round after years of thinking it was flat."

He dropped onto the bed beside her. She rolled onto her back and his gaze traveled over her body. She was all woman, incredibly sexy. He remembered how round and firm her ass had been as he pounded into her from behind.

"Give me a few minutes and I'll give you another geography lesson," he said.

She shifted her head to look at him.

"I thought we were out of condoms."

"We are. But we've still got this." He leaned across and licked one of her nipples.

Her eyelids dropped to half-mast.

"And there's always this." He pressed a kiss to her belly, then the plump rise of her mound.

She held her breath and he glanced up at her. She wanted him again. Just like he wanted her.

"George would have run out of batteries by now. You realize that, don't you?"

She laughed and fisted a hand in his hair, using her grip to draw him back up her body.

"You win. Hands down. Happy?"

"Satisfied, I think you mean."

"Okay, are you satisfied?"

He looked at her body, remembering the too-brief taste he'd had of her earlier.

"Not yet," he said. "But I'm working on it."

POPPY WOKE TO THE SOUND of running water. She opened her eyes and frowned at the unfamiliar ceiling. Then memories from last night washed over her like a tsunami.

Right. She'd come to Jake's room. She'd challenged him and he'd taken her up on it and they'd spent the next several hours going to town on each other.

"Oh, God," she whispered, pressing her fingers against her closed eyes.

The things she'd done last night. The things he'd done. The way her body had responded.

What had she been thinking?

But there had been precious little thinking going on. From the moment she'd met him she'd been too aware of him physically. Then she'd caught him looking at her yesterday and understood she could have him. If she wanted him. And she had.

He'd given her more pleasure in one night than all of her other lovers combined. Hell, he even made George look average. She shifted restlessly as she remembered the feel of his hard cock sliding inside her.

The shower shut off and she sat up in bed.

Shit. She didn't know what to say to him. And he was going to be showered and fresh and possibly dressed, and she was lying here, naked and drowsy and stupid.

She scrambled from the bed and grabbed her jeans. Her panties were tangled in one leg. She didn't bother trying to get them on, simply dragged her jeans on and stuffed her panties into her pocket. Her bra was on the floor. She'd just fastened the clasp when the bathroom door opened and Jake entered. His dark hair was wet and sticking up in spikes. A towel rode low on his hips.

The sight of him made her mouth water.

He stopped in his tracks and they stared at each other for a beat. Then she bent and picked up her shirt.

"Sorry. I didn't mean to oversleep. We should probably be on the road by now," she said.

There was a short pause before he answered.

"No worries. We can make up the time during the day. I took a look at the map. What do you say we aim for Gundagai today?" he said, naming a town roughly halfway between Sydney and Melbourne.

"Sure. That sounds good. I'll, um, I'll grab a shower and meet you at the car."

She buttoned her shirt enough for modesty, picked up her shoes and jacket and headed for the door. She didn't breathe easily until she was outside. Then she closed her eyes and groaned.

"You idiot."

She'd never had a one-night stand in her life. Not that she thought sex was a sacred act that could only occur between two people who loved each other or anything like that. It just hadn't ever come up. She'd been so busy training, concentrating on her swimming, that huge aspects of her life had gone unexplored. Like good sex, apparently. And casual sex. Consequently, she was woefully ill-informed on how she should handle herself the morning after. Her bare toes curled into the concrete as she remembered the awkward pause when Jake had emerged from the bathroom. Was she supposed to have been gone? Was that what the shower had been about—to signal to her that the night was over and it was time for her to skedaddle back to her own room?

Good Lord, maybe she shouldn't have even fallen asleep. Maybe she should have gotten dressed and returned to her room at two or three in the morning, whatever time it had been when they'd finally given in to fatigue and stopped having at each other.

She let herself into her room and stripped. Her body felt strange under the shower, oddly sensitive and tender.

She dressed quickly in a pair of black linen drawstring pants and a white T-shirt. She finger combed her hair, then took a moment to study her face in the mirror.

She didn't look any different, but she felt it. Last night had been a revelation, pure and simple. She felt as though she'd been granted membership to a secret club. For years she'd read books and watched movies where people did crazy, hurtful, risky things for love and lust. She'd never understood why. Until now.

She could understand why a woman would risk a lot for another night in Jake Stevens's arms. The pleasure he'd given her last night was like a drug. She'd never felt more alive, more sensual, more passionate, more beautiful.

And it's never going to happen again.

She knew the practical voice in her head was right. Not for a second did she believe that what had happened between her and Jake was the beginning of something and not the sum total of it. She only hoped she could remember that for the next however many hours she was stuck in the car with him because thinking about him, about what had happened between them last night, made her want him all over again.

He was leaning against the car when she exited her room

with her overnight bag in hand. His arms were crossed over his chest and he had his sunglasses on. Her gaze dropped to his thighs for a second and she remembered the power of him as he'd thrust into her last night.

Never going to happen.

She had to keep reminding herself. She pulled her own sunglasses from her coat pocket and slid them on.

"Ready to go?" he asked.

"Yeah. We can grab breakfast on the road."

"Good idea."

He took the first turn behind the wheel. She cranked the passenger seat back and pretended to be getting a little extra shut-eye. Anything to avoid looking at him and remembering.

He spoke after an hour. "There's a truck stop coming up. You hungry?"

"Sure," she said.

They parked between two huge rigs and made their way inside the Do Drop In Tasty Stop. Jake slid into one side of a booth, she the other. The table was so narrow their knees bumped beneath it.

"Sorry," they both said at the same time.

Poppy studied Jake from beneath her eyelashes. She didn't know how to deal with him now. Before last night, he'd been her enemy and it had been easy to keep her guard up. Yesterday, they'd brokered a peace deal during the long hours on the road. And last night…well, last night they'd crossed the line, and she had no idea how to uncross it.

Right now, for example, she couldn't seem to stop herself from eyeing his broad shoulders and the firm, curved muscles of his pecs as he sat opposite her. He'd felt so hot and hard pressed against her. His skin was smooth and golden and she'd licked and kissed and sucked him all over until he'd—

"What are you having?" Jake asked.

She tore her eyes from his chest and saw that a waitress was hovering beside their booth, pen poised over her pad.

"Um, scrambled eggs on toast. Bacon. Coffee," she said.

"Same." Jake handed his menu to the waitress.

His blue eyes settled on her once they were alone. She remembered the way he'd looked into her eyes, his nose just an inch from her own last night after he'd made her lose her mind the first time.

"Looks like it's going to be another hot day," he said.

"Yep."

"Should grab some water for the road."

"Good idea."

Silence fell. She ran her thumbnail along the edge of the Formica table. If she was more experienced in the ways of the world, she'd know how to handle this situation.

But she wasn't, and she didn't.

They ate in silence, both of them staring out the window at the unexciting panorama of freeway, gas station and dry scrubland.

"I'll get this. You got dinner," she said when the waitress presented their bill.

"If that's what you want," he said.

She stared at him for a moment, frustration twisting inside her. What she wanted was for things to not be so awkward. She frowned as she registered the dishonesty of her thoughts. Okay, that wasn't what she *really* wanted. What she really wanted was for Jake to kiss her again and slide his hand between her legs and make her feel as liquid and hot as she had last night. But she would settle for not feeling stiff and uncomfortable and self-conscious around him.

It was just sex, she reminded herself. *Two adults enjoying each other's bodies. No big deal. Nothing to get your knickers in a knot over.*

She settled the bill and joined Jake at the car.

He'd bought a couple of bottles of water from the gas station and he handed her one. She settled in her seat and closed her eyes once they were on the highway again. If she could doze, it would help pass the time. And maybe a miracle would occur while she slept and she'd wake up and the tension in the car would be gone.

Her thoughts were too chaotic to be restful, however. She could smell Jake's aftershave, could remember washing it from her skin this morning. From her neck and her breasts. From between her thighs.

She pushed the memory away, deliberately focusing instead on Uncle Charlie's upcoming birthday. She thought about her present, tried to work out what to say when she gave it to him. More than anyone else in her life, he'd shaped her to be the person she was today. She didn't have the words to tell him how important he was to her, but somehow she had to find them.

She woke to the sensation of the car slowing.

"Ready to swap?" she asked, sitting up and stretching.

"Pit stop," Jake said. He indicated the toilet block in the rest area they'd pulled into.

She got out of the car and shoved her sunglasses into her pocket. She cracked the seal on her bottle of water as he walked across the gravel to the facilities. She took a mouthful and shielded her eyes to look out across the plains. The land looked brown and dry, unwelcoming.

Gravel crunched as Jake returned. He stopped in front of her and she offered him the water.

"Thanks."

He pushed his sunglasses on top of his head and took a long pull. She let her eyes slide over his chest and belly and thighs. She was gripped with a sudden urge to put her hand on his chest so she could feel the warm, strong resilience of his muscles.

Stop it. She curled her hands into fists, but she couldn't make herself look away.

He took the bottle from his mouth and a single drop of water slid over his lower lip and down his chin. She stared at his mouth, remembering what he'd done to her with his lips and his tongue and his hands last night.

She could feel her nipples hardening. From a look, a single small moment. She met his eyes. For a long beat, neither of them moved. She held her breath.

"Better hit the road." His voice sounded rough.

She climbed into the car and fastened her seat belt. She took a deep breath, then another. She'd never had to fight lust before. She wasn't quite sure how to do it. She was so damned aware of him, couldn't stop remembering small, breathless moments from last night: his harsh breathing near her ear as he pumped into her; the feel of his firm, muscular butt beneath her hands; the skilled flick of his tongue between her legs.

Stop it, she told herself again. She was practically panting. She had to get a grip.

The car dipped as Jake got in beside her and slid his sunglasses onto his face. He started the car and stepped on the gas. Almost immediately he slammed on the brakes. She looked across at him, surprised. He was staring straight ahead, his forehead creased into a frown.

"What's wrong?" she asked.

He turned to look at her. She couldn't see his eyes behind his dark glasses, but something—some instinct—made her look down.

He had a hard-on. The ridge of it was unmistakable beneath his jeans.

"Oh." She let her breath out in a rush, hugely relieved that the need throbbing low in her belly was not one-sided.

"Why didn't you say so?" she said. "I've never done it in a car before."

A slow smile curved his mouth. "Another first. We're really clocking them up."

He leaned across the hand brake and she met him halfway. His lips, his tongue, his heat—just the taste of him sent her pulse through the roof. Within minutes they were pulling at each other's clothes and breathing heavily.

"You stay where you are," she said when they both tried to clamber across the center console at once. She wriggled out of her trousers and underwear while he cranked his seat back. She climbed across the hand brake and into his lap. His erection sat hard and proud beneath her. She shifted her hips, rubbing herself against his length.

"Damn it," she said suddenly. "No protection."

How could she have forgotten something so fundamental?

Jake gave her a wicked smile and reached for the glove box. She shook her head when he pulled out a pack of twelve condoms.

"A little cocky, don't you think?" she said, arching an eyebrow.

"A lot cocky," he said. He grinned and she found herself laughing.

She pulled a condom from the pack and tilted her hips to access his erection. The latex went on smoothly, all the way to his thick base. She held him there and rubbed herself back and forth across the plump head of his cock.

"That feels so good," she said, eyes half shut.

He grabbed her hips and pulled her down impatiently, thrusting upward at the same time. She bit her lip as he filled her. And then she was riding him, his hands on her breasts, his eyes on hers as she drove them both wild.

They came together, bodies shuddering. Poppy braced her arms on the seat on either side of his body afterward, her breath coming in gasps as she stared down at him.

Every time was better than the last. She wasn't sure how that was possible, but it was.

A semitrailer drove past and gave a long blast on its air-horn. They both startled, then laughed.

"Guess we're lucky he wasn't a few minutes earlier," she said, even as she was wondering at her own audacity.

Last night she'd had her first one-night stand and today she'd graduated to sex in a public highway rest stop. She felt as though she'd taken a crash course in sexual desire. Lust 101.

She slid off him and back to her side of the car. Jake took care of the condom, exiting the car to walk back to the toilet block. She struggled into her clothes, bumping elbows and knees in the cramped quarters.

It occurred to her then that, technically, what had just happened between them meant last night had not been a one-night stand.

She tightened the drawstring on her linen pants, frowning. She wasn't sure how to feel about the realization. Clearly, she and Jake had some pretty serious sexual chemistry going on. And they were stuck with each other for at least another day. Her thoughts raced ahead to tonight, to what might happen when they stopped and checked in to yet another motel. Would they pay for one room, or two?

Movement caught the corner of her eye and she turned to watch Jake walk back to the car.

It might be foolish, but she wanted more of him, more of how she felt when she was with him. If he asked—and she hoped he did—she'd opt for one room.

Jake slid behind the wheel. She smiled. He looked at her for a moment, his expression unreadable, then he reached for the ignition key. He didn't turn it. Instead, he took a deep breath and twisted to face her.

"We should probably talk," he said.

"Okay." Suddenly she felt incredibly transparent, as though he knew exactly what she'd been thinking as she watched him walk to the car.

"I'm not really sure how to say this…so I'll just say it. I'm not looking for a relationship right now," he said.

She took a deep breath. Wow. Talk about straight to the point.

"Sure. I know that," she said.

And she did. Just because she'd been thinking about sharing a room with him tonight didn't mean she thought this thing had a future. It was just sex. Nothing more.

"I wanted to be clear. I like you, Poppy. I don't want things to get messy between us, given the way we started out."

"I'm not going to start stalking you and stewing small animals on your stove, if that's what you're worried about," she said. "I had fun last night. But I know exactly what it was."

He studied her face for a long moment, as though he was trying to gauge the truth of her words. She smiled, then punched him on the arm. "Relax. I didn't think you were about to propose because you gave me a bunch of orgasms."

Finally he smiled. "Okay. Good. Great."

He started the car. She put her sunglasses on and made a big deal about getting comfortable in her seat. She stared out the side window as he accelerated onto the highway.

She could punch him on the arm and play it cool however much she liked, but she couldn't lie to herself.

She was disappointed.

It's the sex. You're disappointed there won't be any more of the amazing sex when you stop tonight.

It was true, but it was also a lie. She liked him. She hadn't realized how much until thirty seconds ago.

She crossed her arms over her chest. The sooner they got to Melbourne, the better.

5

JAKE'S CONSCIENCE WAS CLEAR. He'd looked Poppy in the eye and been honest. Admittedly, that had happened *after* he'd had the best quickie of his life with her, but he'd never claimed to be perfect.

Jake reached for his bottle of water and took a mouthful.

He had no idea why he was feeling guilty. She'd wanted it, too. She'd been more than ready to meet him halfway. And she'd been fast to acknowledge that what had happened last night and five minutes ago didn't have a future. No matter how spectacular the sex was.

So why did he feel like a horny teenager desperately trying to justify bad behavior to himself?

There were many solid, rational reasons why nothing beyond sex was ever going to happen between them. They worked together, for starters. And he'd made himself a promise not to get involved with anyone until he'd finished his second novel. The last thing he needed right now was the distraction of a new relationship, especially one with a woman like Poppy.

She'd expect things from him. Commitment being at the top of the list. His thoughts turned to Marly and the mess of their marriage. No way did he want to go there again. Ever. Which didn't leave a man and a woman much room to maneuver, at the end of the day.

He rolled his shoulders and eased his grip on the steering wheel. How in the hell had he gotten from vague guilt about a rest-stop quickie to thoughts of marriage and monogamy?

He slid a glance Poppy's way. She was staring out the window, her face angled away from him.

He thought about the dazed look in her eyes after they'd had sex last night. He remembered her laughter in the bath, and the way he'd caught her scrambling into her clothes this morning.

He was a moron.

He should never have touched her. He should have taken a deep breath last night and walked away instead of letting his hard-on do the thinking for him.

He reached out and punched the radio on, frustrated with himself. Dolly Parton's voice filled the car, wailing about eyes of green and someone stealing her man.

He sighed. What was with rural Australia and country music? Hadn't anyone heard of good old-fashioned rock'n'roll out here in the back of beyond?

The electronic ring of a cell phone cut into Dolly's refrain. Poppy stirred and reached into the backseat to pull her phone from her coat pocket. He tried not to notice the fact that her breast brushed his shoulder or that she smelled good, like sunshine and fresh air.

"Hey, Mom, what's up?" she said into the phone.

He punched off the stereo to make it easier for her to hear.

"What? No!"

He glanced across at her. She'd gone pale and her hand clutched the cell. He eased off the gas.

Something was wrong.

"No! He was fine when I spoke to him on Saturday. He was fine!" she said. Her voice broke on the last word.

Something was definitely wrong. Her eyes were squeezed

tightly shut and she bowed her head forward, pressing a hand to her forehead.

"Did they say… Did they say if he was in any pain? Was it quick?"

Jesus. A death.

He glanced around, but there was no rest area in sight. He pulled off the highway anyway, as far over on the gravel shoulder as he could go.

She didn't seem to notice. All her attention was focused on the bad news coming down the line.

"I understand. Yes. I'll be there as soon as I can. No, I'll drive myself. No. Yes. Okay, I'll…I'll see you soon."

She ended the call and simply sat there, shoulders hunched forward, hands loose between her legs. For a long moment there was nothing but the sound of her breathing and the tick, tick of the engine cooling. A truck sped past and their rental car rocked in its wake.

"Poppy. Is there anything I can do?" he asked quietly.

She didn't say a word, just reached for the door handle and shot from the car. She struck out into the drought-browned pasture alongside the highway as though she could outrun the reality of what she'd learned. Then she stopped suddenly, doubling over. He didn't need to hear her or see her face to know she was crying. She sank to the ground, her shoulders shaking.

Damn.

He had no clue what to do or say. No idea who had died. Her mother had called. Had her father died? Or a brother?

He shook his head and climbed out of the car. He walked slowly toward her, his gut tensing as he saw how tightly she had folded into herself, her arms wrapped tightly around her pulled-up legs, her face pressed into her knees.

He crouched down beside her and placed a hand in the middle of her back.

"Poppy."

She didn't lift her head. He sat down properly, keeping his hand on her back. After a few minutes, she shifted a little and her head came up.

Her eyes were puffy and red, her face streaked with tears. She looked gutted, utterly stricken.

"Uncle Charlie," she said. "Uncle Charlie died."

"I'm sorry."

Talk about inadequate. But there were no words that could take away her pain.

"It was his seventieth on Wednesday. That was why I wanted to get home so badly. He had a heart attack, Mom said."

"Sounds like it was quick."

Her face crumpled. "I should have been there. He was always there for me."

She started crying again. He gave in to his instincts and slid his arm all the way around her shoulders, pulling her against his chest. She let her head flop onto his shoulder and one of her hands curled into his T-shirt and fisted into the fabric. He held her as her body shook.

She was heartbroken. He didn't know what to do for her.

A few minutes later, she loosened her grip on his T-shirt and pulled away from him. He let his arm fall from her shoulders. She used her hands to wipe the tears from her cheeks, not looking at him. She took a couple of long, shuddering breaths. Then she stood.

"I need to get home," she said, still not looking at him.

"Okay. We're nearly to Sydney. We can cut around the city, be in Melbourne in about eleven hours."

He'd already done the math in his head, worked out the best route.

She nodded and started toward the car. She got in and stared straight ahead as he walked to the driver's side. He could almost feel her sucking her emotions back in, building a wall around herself until she could find a safe place to give vent to her grief.

She didn't say a word as they drove around the outskirts of Sydney. She lay on the half-reclined seat facing the window, her back to him. He had no idea if she was crying or sleeping or simply grieving.

He stopped in Goulburn, two hours south of Sydney, for food. She didn't touch her cheeseburger and he wrapped it up and put it aside in case she wanted it later. He stopped again in Albury for gas and coffee. She left the car and walked slowly toward the restrooms, her head down. When she returned her hair was wet and he guessed she'd splashed her face with water.

"I'll drive if you're tired," she offered. Her eyes were bloodshot and blank.

"I'm fine. Three more hours and we'll be home."

She nodded. "Thanks. I appreciate it."

He shrugged off her gratitude. He only wished there was more he could do or say, but they hardly knew each other. Sad, but true.

IT WAS DARK WHEN Jake pulled into the rental car return lot at Melbourne airport. Poppy had been sitting upright and staring grimly out the windshield for the last hour. He could almost hear her making plans in her head.

"Where's home? Can I drop you anywhere?" he asked as they collected their things from the trunk.

"My car's in long-term parking, and my parents are in Ballarat. Uncle Charlie lives— His house is down the road from them."

"Okay. I'll take care of the car return. You get going."

"Thank you. I owe you."

"No, you don't."

Even though he figured she probably didn't want him to, he pulled her close for a quick hug. She was hurting. He felt for her. Surely even a one-night stand and a work colleague was allowed to care that much?

She didn't meet his eyes when the embrace ended, just nodded her head and turned away. He watched her walk toward the pickup point for the courtesy bus to long-term parking.

For the first time since he'd met her, she looked small and fragile.

He turned away. She'd be with her family soon. She'd be okay.

POPPY THREW HER OVERNIGHT bag into the back of her Honda. At least the airport was on the right side of the city; she'd be in Ballarat within an hour. Her eyes filled with tears as she climbed behind the wheel.

Uncle Charlie was dead. She still couldn't comprehend it. It was too big. Too hard. She didn't want it to be true. Didn't want to accept that she would never hear his voice or hold his hand or feel the rasp of his stubble on her cheek when she embraced him.

She blinked the tears away. She couldn't give in and cry yet. She needed to get home. Then she could curl up in a ball and howl the way she wanted to.

She slid her key into the ignition and turned it. Instead of the reassuring roar of the engine starting, she heard a faint click. She frowned and tried the ignition a second time. Again she heard nothing but a faint click.

She stared at her dash and saw that the battery indicator light was shining.

She sat back in her seat. Her battery was dead.

Shit.

Tears came again. She swiped them away with the back of her hand and pulled her cell phone from her pocket. The auto club people could jump-start her. Or if worse came to worst, she could rent another car.

She got out of the car while she was waiting for the phone to connect to the auto club. Might as well look under the hood in case one of the clamps had slipped off a battery terminal or something.

She knew it was a faint hope. She listened to cheery hold music as she peered at her engine. It was hard to tell in the dark, but everything looked the way it should.

"Thank you for calling the Royal Auto Club of Victoria. How can we help you?"

Poppy leaned against the side of her car and explained her situation to the woman. Her eyes were sore and she rubbed them wearily.

"We'll have someone out to take a look at your car as soon as possible," the woman said.

"How long will that be?"

She wanted to be home. She *needed* to be home.

"At this stage, the system is telling me there's a two-hour wait. Our nearest mechanic is on the other side of the city, I'm afraid."

Poppy closed her eyes. Two hours.

"Forget about it. I'll take care of it myself." She ended the call.

She'd go and rent a vehicle. She didn't care about anything else. Her car could sit here until the end of time for all she cared.

A low, dark sports car cruised past, its engine a muted rumble. She grabbed her bag from the backseat and walked around to the front of her car to close the hood.

"What's wrong?"

She slammed the hood down. Jake was standing in the open doorway of the sports car, a frown on his face.

"Dead battery."

"Right." He checked his watch. "What are you going to do?"

She shouldered her bag and used her remote to lock her car.

"The auto club wait is two hours. I'm going to rent a car."

He frowned. "They're pretty busy in there. The strike's still on."

She shrugged. She'd get a freaking taxi all the way if she had to.

"Get in," he said.

She stared at him. "What?"

"I'll take you. Get in."

"It's an hour's drive out of the city."

"So what? You need to get home, right?"

She stared at him.

He was offering only because he felt sorry for her. And things were awkward between them.

But she really needed to get home.

"Okay." Pride was a luxury she couldn't afford right now.

He took her bag and put it in the trunk. She slid into the passenger seat.

"You've been driving for hours," she said when he got in beside her.

"One more hour won't make a difference. If I look like I'm dozing off, feel free to slap me."

She studied his profile as he navigated his way out of the parking lot.

"You didn't have to do this," she said after a short silence.

"I know. I'm a saint."

"Well, I appreciate it. And the fact that you did all the driving today," she said.

"If you're about to thank me for sleeping with you, you can get out now."

It was so unexpected she laughed.

"What's the best route out of the city?" he asked.

She gave him directions. He hit a switch and the mellow sounds of Coldplay eased into the car.

He didn't talk for the next half hour. She was grateful, just as she'd been grateful for his silence earlier today. She wasn't up to polite chitchat, and she wasn't ready to talk about Uncle Charlie. Certainly not to Jake Stevens. He was a virtual stranger, despite how intimate they'd been. There was no way she could share her pain and grief with him.

The exit for Ballarat came up quickly and she gave Jake directions to her parents' house. They lived on the outskirts of the rural center of Ballarat in a big, rambling farmhouse at the end of a long gravel drive. Jake's car dipped and rocked over the uneven ground as they covered the last few yards to the house. The porch light came on as she climbed out of the car. Her parents stood silhouetted in the light.

"You made good time," her mom said.

"We weren't expecting you for a while yet," her father said.

Poppy stood at the bottom of the steps, staring up at them. All the grief she'd held on to for so many hours rose up the back of her throat. She started to cry.

"Oh, Poppy. I knew you'd take it hard," her mother said.

Her mother embraced her with the awkward stiffness that characterized all their physical contact. Vaguely, Poppy was aware of her father introducing himself to Jake and of her mother shuffling her into the house. Then she was sitting at the kitchen table, a cup of sweet tea in her hands, tears still coursing down her face.

"He went the way he always wanted to go—quickly, not hanging around," her father said. "You know he dreaded having a stroke and lingering."

Her parents stood at the end of the table, concern and confusion on their faces. They didn't know what to do. They never did when it came to the world of the emotions.

Never had Poppy needed Uncle Charlie more.

She ducked her head, the tears falling from her chin to plop onto the tabletop.

"She's exhausted. We've been driving for hours," someone said, and she realized Jake was standing behind her.

For some reason it made the tears flow faster and she hunched further into herself.

"Sweetheart. I hate to see you so upset. Uncle Charlie had a good life. We're all going to miss him, but we all have to die sometime. Human beings are mortal creatures, after all," her mother said.

Poppy lifted her head, trying to articulate the gaping sense of loss she felt. "He was my best f-friend."

"I know. And he was my brother and it's very sad but you'll make yourself sick getting so wound up like this," her father said.

Poppy pressed the heels of her hands into her eyes. They didn't understand. They never had.

"What about a shower?" her mother suggested. "What about a shower and some sleep?"

"That's a good idea. What do you say, Poppy?" her father said heartily.

"Sure." Poppy stood and made her way to the bathroom

at the rear of the house. Her mother pressed a fresh towel into her hands.

"I'll turn down your bed," she said, patting Poppy's arm.

Poppy nodded. Then she was alone, the towel clutched to her chest.

She undressed slowly and leaned against the shower wall as the water ran over her, lifting her face into the spray so that she had to gasp through her mouth to breathe. A hundred memories flashed across the movie screen of her mind as the water beat down on her.

Uncle Charlie hooting and hollering from the stands at her first Commonwealth Games. Uncle Charlie sitting patiently beside the pool during her early-morning practice sessions, day after day after day. Uncle Charlie holding her hand in the specialist's office when she was waiting to hear the verdict on her shoulder injury.

She didn't bother drying herself off when she stepped out of the shower. She simply pulled on her old terry-cloth bathrobe and wrapped the towel around her wet hair.

The light was on in her old bedroom and she walked slowly toward it. She pulled up short when she heard her mother talking to someone.

"Don't be ridiculous. It's late, you've been driving for hours. I won't have an accident on my conscience."

Poppy moved to the doorway. Jake stood beside her old bed, watching her mother fluff the pillows. He looked bemused, like a man who didn't quite know what had hit him.

"I'm insisting that Jake stay the night," her mother said when she saw Poppy.

Jake's expression was a masterpiece of tortured middle-class politeness.

"I've just been explaining to your mother that my fishing buddy is expecting me. And that the last thing you probably want is me in your bed after the day you've had." He widened his eyes meaningfully.

"And I've been telling Jake that Allan and I aren't old-fashioned about these kinds of things."

Poppy stared at her mother, not quite getting it. Then her slow brain caught up—her mother thought Jake was her boyfriend.

No wonder he was looking so hunted.

"Jake and I aren't together."

"Oh!" Her mother blushed, one hand pressed to her chest. "I'm so sorry! I just assumed…"

"Jake was helping me out," Poppy said. She turned to him. "She's right, though. You should stay. You must be exhausted after all that driving. There are plenty of other bedrooms."

"Yes! Of course there are! Adam's room is right next door, and the bed is already made up." Her mother nodded effusively, eager to make up for her gaffe.

"I'm fine. Really," Jake said.

Poppy's mother looked to her, clearly expecting her to intervene.

Poppy shrugged. "It's your decision," she said, turning away.

He was a grown-up. If he thought he was okay to drive, it was up to him. She sat on the side of the bed and stared at her feet. She was numb and exhausted and so empty it hurt.

There was a short silence.

"Maybe I should get a few hours' shut-eye before I hit the road again," Jake said.

Poppy pulled the quilt back and crawled beneath the covers. She didn't look at either of them, just rolled onto her side and closed her eyes.

She wanted to wipe the day out, strike it from the record as though it had never happened. She wanted to turn back the clock to a time when Uncle Charlie was still a part of her world.

"I'll show you Adam's room," she heard her mother say.

There was the scuff of shoes on floorboards, then Poppy was alone. She opened her eyes and stared blindly at the far wall.

"Uncle Charlie," she whispered.

JAKE LAY IN POPPY'S brother's bed and stared at the ceiling. By rights he should be halfway to Melbourne by now, Poppy and her grief left far behind. Instead he was lying here, listening to the sounds of a strange house settling for the night.

The truth was, he hadn't been able to leave her.

Which was nuts. Even if she was devastated by grief, the last person Poppy would turn to was him. They'd been thrown together by circumstances, nothing else. Even the sex had been about availability and proximity. At least initially, anyway. And yet here he was in her parents' house, unable to abandon her to her family's distant, entirely inadequate sympathy.

His chest got tight every time he remembered the empty, sad look on Poppy's face as she sat at her parent's kitchen table, shoulders hunched forward as though making herself smaller could diminish her grief, protect her from it somehow. And her parents had simply stood there and let her ache.

His own family were far from perfect. His father had a temper and his mother wasn't above playing the martyr to get her own way. His brothers and sisters all had their fair share of flaws and foibles. And yet if someone close to them had died, if one of them was hurting or needy or in trouble, the Stevens family would not hesitate to circle the wagons and pull up the drawbridge. Hugs would be the order of the day, along with kisses and tears and laughter. It would be messy and loud and warm and real.

By contrast, Yvonne Birmingham had looked so uncomfortable embracing her daughter that she might as well have been undergoing root canal, while Allan had offered his grief-stricken daughter rational words and philosophy and precious little else. Jake had waited in vain for someone to offer Poppy the simple comfort of another warm body to cling to. Hell, even a hand on the shoulder and a sympathetic handkerchief or tissue would have done the trick. But the Birminghams were not huggers, he'd quickly realized.

Allan had given Jake their bona fides while Poppy was in the shower—they were both academics, tenured professors at Ballarat University. Allan taught history, Yvonne English literature. Jake had detected a faint accent in both their speeches and he guessed from the photographs on the wall that they had emigrated to Australia from England some years ago.

He couldn't think of a more unlikely pair to have produced a larger-than-life, earthy woman like Poppy. In fact, the more he thought about it, the more impossible it seemed. They were so self-contained and cerebral, and Poppy was so physical and full of energy and honesty.

Staring into the dark, he pondered what it must have been like for Poppy, growing up with parents who lived in their minds when she was a person who lived in her belly and heart. He might not know all the ins and outs of Poppy's world, but he knew that much about her.

Lonely, he guessed. Hence her close relationship with Uncle Charlie.

The second cup of tea Yvonne had pressed on him before bed made its presence felt and he swung his legs over the side of the mattress and went in search of the bathroom. He made a deal with himself as he shuffled up the darkened hallway. He'd try to grab a few hours' sleep when he got back to bed, but if sleep didn't come he'd dress and slip out the back door and head for Melbourne.

It wasn't as though he was serving any purpose here, after all.

He was passing Poppy's bedroom door on the way back to Adam's room when a low sound made him pause. He gritted his teeth; she was crying. He hesitated for only a second. He could be a stubborn bastard and a self-confessed smart-ass, but it simply wasn't in him to walk away from someone in so much pain.

He pushed her door open. "Poppy."

She didn't respond but he could hear her breathing.

Again he hesitated. Then he entered the room and closed the door. His shin found her bed before his outstretched hands did and he swore under his breath.

"Don't freak out, I'm getting into the bed," he said.

She didn't say a word as he pulled back the covers. It was only a double bed, but she was curled up on the far side. He slid across the cool sheets until his chest was pressed against her back. He wrapped an arm around her waist and pulled her tightly against his body. She was rigid with tension and as unresponsive as a lump of wood.

"It's okay, Poppy," he said very quietly.

She started to shake. He pulled her closer, curling his legs behind hers so that they were tightly spooned. He could feel her grief, her pain, vibrating through her.

"It's okay," he said again.

"No, it isn't."

Her chest heaved as she sucked in a breath, then she was shuddering, sniffing back tears, gulping for air. He held her tightly, not saying a word. It wasn't as though there was anything to say, anyway. There wasn't a well-formed phrase in the world that made losing someone less sad.

Slowly the crying jag passed. Poppy sniffed noisily and moved restlessly in his arms. He eased away from her and released his grip.

"I'm sorry," she said.

"For what?"

"All of this. My mom forcing you to stay the night. Taking more time away from your fishing trip. This wasn't exactly what you signed on for when you offered me a lift home."

"Your mom didn't force me to stay. I wanted to make sure you were okay."

Her head turned toward him on the pillow. In the faint light from the window he could see the dampness on her cheeks.

"Noble of you."

"Don't worry, I'm sure it won't last."

She managed a faint smile, then she used the sleeve of her robe to wipe her eyes. It was a child's gesture and it made her seem even more vulnerable.

"You want to talk?" he asked. His ex-wife would keel over in shock at hearing those four words leave his mouth, but he didn't know what other comfort to offer.

She shrugged and dabbed at her face again with her sleeve.

"Not much to say. He was my best friend. He taught me how to swim. Came to every major meet and most of the minor ones. And now he's gone."

"He was your father's brother, yeah?"

"Yes. But Charlie was older by twelve years. There was less money when he was born, so he didn't get the same education as my father. He was a house painter. He was the one who decided to emigrate to Australia. Mom and Dad followed him a few years later."

"I wondered about the accent."

"Cambridge."

"Right."

He thought about what she'd said about her uncle coming to every meet and what it implied about her parents—they hadn't. And for the first time it occurred to him that while he'd seen plenty of books piled all over the place and black-and-white photographs of England on the walls of her parents' home, there hadn't been a single shot of Poppy. No photos on the winner's dais. No newspaper clippings. No framed medals or ribbons. No indication at all that the Birminghams had a world-record-holding, gold-medal-winning daughter.

"You know what the crazy thing is?" Poppy asked after a short silence. "All I could think about when we were on the road is getting home. And once I got here, I realized that the thing I'd been holding out for was Uncle Charlie. And he's not here anymore." She tried to keep her voice light, as though she was telling a joke on herself, but there was a telltale quaver in it.

"It was his birthday on Wednesday, too. I'd been teasing him for months about what I was going to get him. And now he'll never know…" She was crying again, tears sliding down her face and onto the pillow.

"What did you get him?"

"I had a frame made for my first gold medal. And there was this picture of the two of us when I was a kid… I wanted him to know that I couldn't have done any of it without him."

"It sounds great. I bet he would have loved it."

She shifted, sitting upright then leaning over the side of the bed. He heard the rustle of paper as she fumbled in the dark, then she lifted a large, flat box from beneath the bed. The weight of it landed heavily on his legs as she placed it in his lap.

"Open it," she said.

He stilled. "Are you sure?"

"Yes. I want someone to see it."

There was an undercurrent to her words. Then he remembered the lack of photos in the house and thought he understood.

She flicked on the bedside lamp. They both blinked in the sudden light, even though it wasn't terribly bright. He glanced at her. Her eyes were puffy, her cheeks damp. Her hair had dried into messy spikes. She looked about fifteen years old.

"Open it," she said.

He pulled himself into a sitting position. She'd wrapped the box in shiny black paper with a bright yellow ribbon. He felt as though he was trespassing as he tugged the bow loose and slid his thumb under the flap of the paper.

"Tear it. I don't care," she said when he tried to ease the tape off neatly.

When he continued to be careful, she reached across and ripped the paper for him, shoving it unceremoniously to one side. Then she found the tab that released the lid on the plain packing box beneath and pushed it open. Jake eased a double layer of tissue paper aside to stare at Poppy's gift to her late uncle.

The frame was dark wood—walnut, he guessed—and deep, creating a three-inch recess behind the glass. Poppy's first gold medal was fixed to a dark green mount. A black-and-white photograph sat alongside it. The middle-aged man in the photograph had big shoulders and a craggy face. His dark eyes were gentle as he looked at the little girl standing beside him in the shallow end of the pool. She had short blond hair and two teeth missing from the front of her smile. And she looked up at him with absolute trust and adoration as he guided her arms into position.

Poppy sniffed loudly.

"He was so patient with me. He never got angry with me, except when I doubted myself," she said. "He loved swimming, couldn't get enough of it. Knew all the coaches, all my competitors' stats."

She shook her head. "I can't explain it."

"You don't need to. You loved him. And he loved you."

"Yes. He did."

Her chin wobbled as she reached out to press her fingers to the glass over her uncle Charlie's face.

"I'm going to miss him so much."

Jake slid his arm around her shoulders and pulled her against his chest. She didn't resist, didn't try to be strong. Her hands curled into the muscles of his shoulders and she pressed her face into his chest. Her breath came in choppy bursts and her tears were warm on his skin.

He eased against the pillows, one hand smoothing circles on her back. With the light on he could see more of her room. The far wall was covered in ragged posters of past Australian swimming greats—Dawn Fraser, Shane Gould, Kieren Perkins. A fistful of old swimming carnival ribbons were pinned together in the corner. All blue for first place, naturally. To the side of the bed was a battered dressing table. He couldn't help smiling to himself as he saw the earplugs, goggles, swim caps and other swimming paraphernalia strewn across it. Any other teenager would have loaded it with makeup, perfume and pictures of the latest teen heartthrob, but not Poppy.

"You must be tired," Poppy said after a few minutes. "You've been driving all day. Now you've got me sooking all over you."

"I'm fine."

"Still. You should try to get some sleep. You're going to be on the road again tomorrow, aren't you, driving to hook up with your fishing buddy?"

"Yeah."

She pushed herself away from his chest and reached for the frame. He watched as she set it beside the bed, leaning it against her bedside table. He pushed back the covers and swung his legs over the side of the bed, preparing to return to her brother's room. She frowned.

"What's wrong?" he asked.

"Nothing."

"Poppy."

She lifted a shoulder in a self-conscious shrug. "Would you mind sleeping in here with me? It makes it easier, not being alone."

"Not a problem."

She gave him a watery smile. "Thanks. I appreciate it."

She sat on the edge of the bed and shrugged out of the bathrobe. Then she strode naked across to the dressing table and tugged a drawer open. He told himself to look away, but it was too late—he'd seen the full swing of her naked breasts and the mysterious shadow between her thighs as she bent to pull an old T-shirt from the drawer. He'd traced the firm curve of her ass and the strong lines of her back with his eyes as she tugged the T-shirt over her head.

Only when she was walking back to the bed did he manage to make himself look away. Too late. Way too late.

Despite the fact that he knew it made him a cad of the highest order, he couldn't help responding to what he'd just seen. She had a great body and he'd enjoyed many hours of pleasure with her last night. He told himself she was grieving, in shock, sad. His penis didn't care. It remembered only too well the feel of her skin against his, the slick tightness of her body, the rush of her heated breathing in his ear.

The bed dipped as she got in beside him and flicked off the light. He closed his eyes. There was no way he was going to get any sleep lying here with a hard-on. He resigned himself to a long night.

"Jake. I know this is beyond the call of duty, but would you mind…would you mind holding me?"

Right.

"Um, sure. Not a problem. How do you want me to…?"

"Like you did before was nice." He could hear the shyness in her voice, knew how much it was costing her to ask him for comfort.

"Cool."

She rolled onto her side, her back to him. He reached down and adjusted his hard-on in his boxer briefs in a futile attempt to minimize the obviousness of his arousal. Careful to keep his hips away from her rear, he slid his arm around her torso and pressed his chest against her back.

Funny how last time he'd done this it hadn't been even remotely erotic. But then she'd been wearing the robe and he'd been too focused on how upset she was to register the warmth of her skin and the brush of the lower curve of her breasts against the back of his hand. He hadn't noticed the clean, fresh smell of her or thought for a minute about any of the things they'd done to each other last night. The way she'd taken him in her mouth. The way her eyes had widened when he'd found her sweet spot and touched it just right. The greedy, hungry way she'd reached for his cock and guided him inside her.

He gritted his teeth and forced his mind to something else. The stats for the top five teams on the AFL ladder. The chances of Roger Federer winning both Wimbledon and the U.S. Open again this year. His agent's recent phone message requesting a meeting with him.

Poppy sighed. Jake felt some of the tension leave her body as she relaxed into the bed.

"I really appreciate this, Jake," she said again.

He tightened his grip around her waist in response and she wriggled her backside more closely into the cradle of his hips. She stilled.

So much for his playing the chivalrous knight.

"Is that what I think it is?" she asked.

"Yes. But I would like to point out that sometimes it has a mind of its own. And you have a great body."

She rolled away from him, and he waited for her to kick him out of bed and tell him what an insensitive jerk he was.

"Where are the condoms?" she asked instead.

In the dim light from the partially open curtain he could see her pulling her T-shirt over her head. Any blood that wasn't already there rushed south and his cock grew rock hard. It got even harder when she slid a hand over his belly and into his underwear to wrap her palm around him.

"In the car."

"Huh. We'll have to be careful, then," she said.

Her hand was working up and down his shaft. He closed his eyes. Then his conscience came calling, tap-tapping persistently in the back of his mind.

"Are you sure you want to do this? I mean, you're upset. I don't want you doing anything you might regret."

She pressed a wet, openmouthed kiss to his chest.

"I want to feel alive right now. Do you mind?"

"Do I feel like I mind?"

"No. You feel good." She practically purred the last word.

She slid a leg over both of his and shifted so that she was straddling his hips. She pushed his underwear down and he shoved it the rest of the way down his legs. Then she slid his cock into her wet heat and bore down on him.

"Oh, yeah." He sighed as her body enveloped him.

She started to rock her hips. He could see her breasts swaying in the dim light, pale and full. He slid his hands up her rib cage and took the weight of her in his hands, sliding his thumbs over her nipples. They hardened instantly. She let her head drop back.

She felt so good. Soft yet firm. Silky and smooth. He drew her down so he could pull a nipple into his mouth. She shuddered and began to circle her hips. He slid a hand between their bodies to where they were joined. Her curls were wet and warm and she was swollen with need. He teased her with his thumb, working her gently. She started to pant. He felt her tense around him.

He thrust up into her and wished he could see her face properly. He had to settle for the fierce throb of her muscles tightening around him as she came and the low moan she made in the back of her throat. He closed his eyes and thrust up into her rhythmically, chasing his own release. Then he remembered they didn't have a condom.

Damn.

He stilled, his hands finding her hips to stop her from moving on him.

"No condom," he reminded her. She stilled.

"Right."

She slid off him, one last torturous stroke of her body against his. Before he could feel true regret, she shifted down his body and lowered her head. The wet heat of her mouth encompassed him and he groaned his approval.

She used her hand and her mouth and soon had him bowed with tension. He drove his fingers into her hair and held her head as he came. Afterward, she pressed a kiss onto his belly and rested her cheek on his hip.

"Come back here," he said.

Her body slid along his as she joined him on the pillow. He peered into her face, trying to see her eyes.

"You okay?"

"If you keep asking questions like that, you're going to ruin my image of you as a gifted-yet-emotionally-shallow pants man."

"I'd hate to do that. Not when I've spent so many years perpetuating that image. It's not something that happens overnight, you know."

She smiled. He looked at her and wondered if that was really how she thought of him—a pants man, out for what he could get, when he could get it. Then he thought over the past few years of his life and wondered how inaccurate the description was, at the end of the day.

As a teenager, the idea of being a celebrated swordsman had held enormous appeal. Lots of women, lots of sex, lots of variety. The Errol Flynn myth, basically. But as an adult man, he knew there was more to life than sex.

For a moment he was filled with a bittersweet regret for the early years of his marriage. For moments like these when he and Marly had laughed and talked while their bodies cooled. For the comfort and joy and familiarity of coming home to find the lights on, cooking smells in the kitchen and off-key singing coming from somewhere in the house. For shared jokes and favorite movies and the sense of achievement that came from finding the right birthday or Christmas gift.

But it was impossible to remember the good times without the bad memories crowding in. The bitter fights, the recriminations. The tears, the misery. The fury. The helplessness. And, finally, the emptiness when it was all over.

So, yeah, maybe being described as a pants man wasn't the

highlight of his life, but it beat the hell out of his marriage and his divorce. Hands down.

Poppy's head was heavy on his shoulder and her breathing had deepened. He peered down at her. She was asleep. Exhausted, no doubt, after the trials of the day. Slowly, he eased her head off his shoulder and onto the pillow.

He'd done his bit. He'd offered her all that he had to give. She would wake tomorrow and remember all over again that her uncle Charlie was gone. But she'd gotten through the first night, and she'd get through the rest, too.

His boxer briefs were lost somewhere beneath the quilt. He didn't bother looking for them, just slipped out of bed and back to Poppy's brother's room. He dressed in the dark and let himself out the back door. His car engine sounded loud in the quiet of the country night. He rolled down the driveway, then hit the gas when he reached the road. Before long he was turning onto the freeway toward town.

He spared a thought for how Poppy would feel when she woke. Then he remembered her pants man comment. She'd understand.

6

___

HE WAS GONE. POPPY REGISTERED the cool sheets and the absence of warm male body and lifted her head to confirm that Jake had left her bed.

She rolled onto her back, her forearm draped over her eyes to block out the sunlight shining between the half-open curtains. After a long moment she lifted her arm and squinted at the clock on her bed stand. It was nearly eight. She'd slept all the way through the night, exhausted by grief and a heart-pounding climax courtesy of Jake's clever hands and hard body.

He must have gone back to his own bed. She wished he hadn't. His warmth, the low timbre of his voice, the simple sound of another human being breathing next to her—he'd helped her get through the night.

He'd been kind to her. Very kind. He'd stayed overnight when he hadn't wanted to, he'd sought her out when he'd heard her crying. And he'd held her, offering her the reassurance of his body. And, later, he'd offered her his desire and a few precious moments of forgetfulness and release, too.

She'd called him a pants man afterward. It wasn't true. Men who were just after sex didn't take the time to offer comfort to someone in need.

Jake Stevens was a nice man. It was a surprising discovery, given the way they'd started out.

She pushed her hair off her forehead. It was time to get up. Time to face the day ahead. Her parents. Her brother and sister, most likely. The funeral arrangements.

Her belly tightened at the thought and she took a steadying breath. It was tempting to hide away and grieve. But putting Charlie to rest was the last thing she could do for him.

She rolled out of bed. She kept some old clothes at her parents' place for the weekends when she stayed the night and she pulled on a pair of worn jeans and the T-shirt she'd worn for just a few minutes last night before she'd felt the unmistakable hardness of Jake's erection against the curve of her backside.

Even now, hours later, the memory sent a wash of heat through her. She eyed herself in the dressing table mirror as she finger combed her hair. That was the thing about death—life went on despite it. People ate and slept and fought and laughed and cried and lusted and had sex, same as they always had.

Life went on.

"Uncle Charlie," she said quietly.

The world had not stopped because he was dead, but it had changed for her, irrevocably.

She could hear low conversation as she walked toward the kitchen. She recognized the pitch and rhythms of her sister's speech and the low bass of her brother's. They'd come up from the city, then, as she'd guessed they would.

"I still can't believe I missed him. All this way and he's gone already." This from her sister, sounding aggrieved.

"I thought you came all this way for Uncle Charlie?" Adam said.

Poppy stopped in the doorway. Her mother was at the sink, filling the kettle. Her father hovered over the toaster, eyeing the glowing slots like a cat at a mouse hole. Adam and Gillian sat at the table, the morning papers spread wide before them.

"Poppy. You're up," her mother said too brightly. "I hope you had a good night's sleep."

"It was okay."

Poppy stepped forward to kiss her brother and sister hello. Gillian patted her arm briefly as Poppy pressed a kiss to her cheek.

"How are you holding up?" Gillian asked.

"You know." Poppy shrugged. "Did you two come up together?"

"Yes. I'm due back in the afternoon, but I thought I could help out with the funeral arrangements this morning."

"And meet a certain much-lauded author," Adam said with a dry smile.

Poppy frowned. "Sorry?"

Adam nudged Gillian's chair with the toe of his shoe. They were both small and dark-haired like their parents, dressed expensively and conservatively in dark business suits.

"Mom told Gill that Jake Stevens was here when she called early this morning and she was in the car like a shot," Adam said.

Gillian flushed a little. "Thank you for making me sound like a juvenile delinquent with a crush. I happen to be a great admirer of his work. *The Coolabah Tree* is a modern Australian classic."

Poppy crossed to the cupboard to grab a coffee mug. She should have known her family would be excited about meeting Jake. Her mother had taught a seminar on him a few years ago and her sister worked for a small feminist publishing house in the city.

"I didn't put two and two together until this morning, Poppy," her mother said. "You should have told me who Jake was. I'm so embarrassed I didn't recognize him."

"It wasn't exactly at the top of my mind last night."

"I know, but still…"

Poppy spooned instant coffee into her mug.

"I should go wake him. He probably wants to hit the road."

"Oh, but he's gone already," her mother said. "His car was gone this morning when I let the cats out."

The teaspoon clanged loudly against the side of the mug. Not just gone from her bed, but gone from the house? Gone in the early hours of the morning?

"It was good of him to drive you up here when your car broke down," her father said.

"Yes," Poppy said. She stared at the brown granules in the bottom of the cup. It was ridiculous, but she felt abandoned. As though Jake had offered her something in the dark of the night that he'd reneged on this morning.

"I still can't believe you made that gaffe over the rooms, Mom," Gillian said. She shook her head, a wry smile on her lips.

Adam made a joke at their mother's expense, then her mother asked something about Gillian's work and her father asked who wanted more toast.

A great wave of sadness and loneliness and grief washed over Poppy as she watched her family. She'd never felt like one of them, had always felt like an outsider in the face of their collective academic and professional achievements. It had always been her and Uncle Charlie against the rest of them.

Her vision blurred and her shoulders slumped. Without saying a word, she moved to the back door and pushed her way out into the sunlight.

"Poppy," her mother called after her.

"Let her go," she heard Adam say. "She obviously wants to be alone."

Head down, she walked out into the backyard. She didn't know where she was going. She just knew that it would be

though he was sitting beside her. An increasingly familiar pang of loneliness and sadness pierced her.

His funeral had been exhausting, a day of shaking hands and accepting hugs and condolences, of trying not to cry too much or too loudly. She had been surprised by the turnout, particularly by the number of people from the swimming community who came to pay their respects. Her old coach. Some of her former competitors. Former swimmers from the high school squad Charlie had coached way back in the day. His warmth and wisdom had touched a lot of lives. He'd been valued. He would be missed. And he would be remembered. At the end of the day, that knowledge had given her some solace.

Getting on with the plod of everyday life was hard, however. He had been her mentor, counselor and friend, and she picked up the phone countless times a day to call him and tell him some joke or small story she knew he'd relish, only to remember all over again that he was gone, that there would be no more phone calls or shared laughter.

Her mouth grim, Poppy deleted the paragraph she'd written while Jake hovered over her shoulder. Not gibberish, thank God, but not something she wanted her boss to read, that was for sure. She pushed her hair off her forehead and rolled her shoulders. Then she put her fingers to the keyboard again. This article was due by midday and she still wasn't happy with the intro and the conclusion. She'd sweated over both until late last night, staying at her desk until the cleaners came and began emptying trash and vacuuming around her.

It worried her that the writing wasn't getting any easier. If anything, it felt harder. The more she learned in her night classes, the more she could see the failings in her own work. And the worse thing was, she didn't know how to fix them.

Even though she and Jake were the only people in the department this early, Poppy glanced up as she eased her desk drawer open. It wasn't as though she'd care too much if some-one else saw what she was doing, but if Jake caught sight of the underlined, annotated article in her drawer she didn't think she would ever recover from the humiliation.

He was busy checking his e-mail, one hand idly clicking away at the mouse. The glow from his desk lamp gave his dark hair golden highlights. She switched her attention to the article in her hand.

It had been her class assignment this week—select a piece of journalism she admired and analyze its structure and con-tent. She'd agonized over her choice and then forced herself to admit that the only reason she wasn't selecting one of Jake's articles was because of what had happened between them. Dumb. He was the best writer in the department, one of the most awarded on the paper. And she'd admired him for years. She might feel foolish and naive and exposed be-cause she'd slept with him and allowed herself to hope for more, but it didn't change the fact that he was one of the best. And if she was going to learn, she wanted to learn from the best.

She read his opening paragraph again, admiring the decep-tively easy flow of it. It was impossible to stop at those few sentences, though—inevitably she wanted to keep reading, even though she'd gone over and over the damned thing many times already. He was a master of the hook, superb at deliv-ering information in fresh and interesting ways and drawing the reader in. His observations were insightful, his judgments crisp and unapologetic.

She turned to her own opening paragraph, frowning at the stiffness of her phrasing. No matter what she tried—chatty and informal, choppy and succinct or somewhere in between—

she wound up sounding like a high school student laboring over an end-of-term paper.

The tap-tap of Jake's keyboard had her lifting her head again. Words filled the screen as his fingers flew. For a moment she simply stared at him, envying him his easy gift. He was in his element, utterly confident. She knew what that felt like. At least, she used to know.

She shoved the annotated article into her drawer and pulled her keyboard toward herself. She might not have natural talent, but she was smart and she learned fast. She would conquer this if it killed her.

Just as she would live down making the rookie's mistake of sleeping with a coworker.

LATER THAT AFTERNOON during the department meeting, Jake leaned back in his chair and studied the woman sitting diagonally opposite him. Poppy sat ramrod straight, a pad and pen at the ready in front of her like a good little schoolgirl, just in case Leonard said anything she needed to jot down. Her gaze was resolutely focused on their boss as he droned on and on about circulation figures.

She'd made a point of being everywhere he wasn't since their nonconversation this morning. If he entered the kitchen, she left. If he was collecting something from the printer, she gave it a wide berth. So much for hoping there would be no repercussions from their road-trip fling.

She was pale, he noted, her eyes large in her face. A tuft of hair stuck up on her crown as though she'd been running her fingers through her hair. Her lipstick had worn off, but her lower lip was wet from where she'd just licked it.

She looked sad. And sexy. A disturbing combination at the best of times.

He frowned.

As if she could sense his regard, her gaze flicked up to lock with his. Her face remained expressionless, utterly still for a long five seconds. Then she coolly returned her attention to their boss.

Jake shifted in his seat. He told himself that there was no rational justification for her anger, that he had no reason to feel guilty. He didn't owe her anything, after all. He'd gone beyond the call of duty, driving her home when her car had broken down, hanging around at her parents' place to make sure she was okay.

Yeah, and then you crawled into her bed in the middle of the night when she was at her most vulnerable and threw the leg over.

He would swear on a stack of Bibles that sex had been the last thing on his mind when he'd heard her crying. Absolutely. And yet somehow he'd still ended up shagging her again.

Never screw the crew.

Don't dip your pen in the office ink.

Don't shit in your own nest.

There was a reason there were half a dozen colloquial warnings against sleeping with a coworker—the aftermath sucked.

I was honest with her. I told her I wasn't looking for a relationship.

Which gave him the perfect get-out-of-jail-free card—in theory. Things got a little muddy once he factored in her grief and the way he'd felt compelled to comfort her and the truths they'd shared in the small hours of the morning. Oh, and the sex. The postcomforting, postsharing sex.

He should have said no. Should have ignored his hard-on, rolled out of bed and gone back to her brother's room. Instead, he'd gotten lost in the warmth of her body then bailed without saying goodbye.

He waited until she was filing out of the meeting room with the others before approaching her.

"Poppy, can I have a word?"

Several sets of eyes turned their way and she had no choice but to agree. She hovered near the door as the last person exited.

"What?" she asked.

She crossed her arms over her chest and set her jaw stubbornly. Clearly, she wasn't about to make this easy.

"Look, I would have woken you but I thought you needed the sleep more," he said.

"No, you didn't. You didn't wake me because you were worried I would take what had happened the wrong way."

"Yeah, and I was right, wasn't I?" he said, gesturing to indicate the discussion they were having, their mutually closed-off body language, the tension in the room.

"You're so arrogant it blows my mind," she said, shaking her head. "For your information, you are not God's gift to women. A handful of decent orgasms doesn't even come close to making you irresistible."

He crossed his arms over his chest and leaned his hip against the table. For the first time all day she had some color in her cheeks and there was life in her eyes. He wasn't sure if he should be pleased or not. And whether he should be worried about noticing in the first place.

"Why are you so pissed with me, then?"

"I don't know. Maybe because you sneaked out of my parents' house like a thief in the night?"

"So? You knew I needed to get going, that I wanted to catch up with my buddy. What was the big deal if I left early or not?"

She opened her mouth then shut it without saying anything. Her gaze slid over his shoulder and her jaw tensed. Her eyes were angry when they met his again.

"Fine, I admit it. You're right. I was surprised when you weren't there in the morning. I thought at the very least that we were friends after everything that had happened. That you cared enough to say goodbye. I felt stupid when I realized you were gone."

He stared at her. Her confronting honesty left him nowhere to go. It was his turn to look away. "We both agreed that it was just sex."

"I know."

And they both knew it had become more than sex when he slid into her bed and wrapped his arms around her.

"I'm sorry," he said after a long silence. "I only wanted to help. I didn't mean to hurt you."

"I'm not crying myself to sleep over you, Stevens," she said drily. "Get over yourself."

He shrugged. "For what it's worth, I'm a shit prospect anyway. Workaholic. Messy. Hopeless with birthdays and anniversaries. Cranky in the mornings."

She simply looked at him, her big gray eyes depthless. "Are we done here?"

"Yeah, we're done."

She walked away, her spine very straight. He watched till she turned the corner, aware that he still felt dissatisfied, as though they had unfinished business.

What had he expected from their confrontation, anyway? What exactly had he been trying to achieve?

He remembered the way they'd sparred in the car, the push and pull of their conversation over dinner at the steak house. He remembered her laugh, the deep throaty pleasure of it.

And he remembered the utter vulnerability of her as she wept in his arms.

He liked Poppy Birmingham. Hell, he even admired her, especially after meeting her parents and gaining a small glimpse into the indifference she'd had to fight against to rise to the top of her sport. If he hadn't messed things up by sleeping with her, he'd like to think they could have been friends.

But he had. And, worse yet, he still wanted her, even though he knew he was never going to have her again.

JAKE LEFT THE DEPARTMENT earlier than usual that night. His agent had called to set up a meeting, and Jake had been unable to put him off any longer. Poppy was still at her desk, bent over her keyboard, one hand absently combing her hair into spikes. She worked long hours. He wondered if journalism was living up to her expectations.

His agent was waiting for him at the wine bar in the nearby restaurant precinct of Southgate when Jake arrived. Dean Mannix waved a hand when he spotted Jake but didn't bother standing. Nearly sixty years old, he had bad knees and walked with the aid of a cane. His improbably black hair gleamed with hair oil and Jake pretended not to notice the discreet touch of eyeliner around the other man's eyes.

"Where's Rambo?" he asked, glancing around for his agent's much-cosseted Chihuahua.

"Spa day," Dean said with the flick of a limp wrist.

"Ah. What are you drinking?" Jake asked, seeing Dean's glass was almost empty.

"Surprise me with something sweet and sticky."

Jake suppressed a smile and crossed to the bar. It had been nearly twelve months since he and Dean had spoken face-to-face. In the early days, his agent had practically lived on his doorstep. Marly had called him "that little man" and rolled her eyes every time he called. But there hadn't been much need for Dean to make contact recently.

Jake scanned the cocktail menu and ordered a Fluffy Duck and a glass of merlot. Dean's mouth quirked into a smile when he saw the umbrella poking out the side of his drink.

"Fabulous." He took a long pull from the straw. "And absolutely disgusting."

He said it with such relish Jake could only take it as high praise.

"So, what's up?" Jake asked.

He waited for Dean to ask him about his writing, when Jake might have something for him. That was usually why Dean requested a face-to-face.

"Did I mention I saw Bryce Courtney the other day?" Dean said instead. He went on to tell an anecdote about the other author. Jake listened and made the appropriate noises, growing more and more tense with every passing minute. Finally Dean drank the last of his cocktail and sat back in his chair.

"Isn't this the part where you ask me what I've been working on and I lie and tell you I've got a good start on something?" Jake joked.

Dean smiled but his eyes were sad.

"Jake, I'm going to let you off the hook," he said. "Make it official and tear up our agreement."

Jake let his breath out on a rush. This was the last thing he'd been expecting. "You're cutting me loose? You don't want to represent me anymore?"

"I'd love to represent you. I think you're a wonderful, talented writer and you've made me a lot of money. I've been proud to have your name on my books for the past seven years. But the truth is that you aren't writing anything for me to represent."

"So I'm a little blocked. I've got the second book outlined, the broad strokes are there. I just need a clean run at it."

"Jake, it's been seven years. And, yes, I know things with Marly were messy for the first two years, but you've had five years since the divorce and you haven't brought me anything."

Jake stared at him, unable to refute his words. "So I'm deadwood now? You're just going to cut me off?"

Dean sighed heavily. "No. Like I said, I'm letting you off the hook. No expectations. No guilt. No niggle in the back of your mind. You're free to write or not write as you choose. No pressure from anyone but yourself."

"Wow. I feel so free. What a gift you've given me."

Dean didn't flinch at his sarcasm and Jake immediately felt like an asshole. It wasn't as though Dean hadn't been patient. Seven years was a long leash by anyone's standards. Jake rubbed a hand over his face.

"Sorry. I just…I understand. You've been very patient."

"You start writing again, call me. Call me anyway, let me know how you're doing," Dean said.

Jake forced a smile. "Sure."

Dean leaned forward. "I know you've got another book in you, Jake, but you need to give yourself permission to write it."

Jake frowned. "What the hell is that supposed to mean?"

"Why do you think you haven't been able to get the words down?"

"I've been busy. I've let other things get in the way. No discipline."

"You know what I think? I think Marly spent so much time blaming you for being away on a book tour when she miscarried that you couldn't help but absorb some of it. And now you won't let yourself write again because giving up something you loved is your way of punishing yourself."

Jake flinched. "Didn't realize you'd hung up your shingle as a headshrinker since we last saw each other, mate. Or have you just been watching too much *Dr. Phil?*"

"Something has held you back all these years."

"I don't need counseling, for Christ's sake. I need an agent."

Dean braced his arms on the table and pushed himself to his feet.

"When you need an agent, you'll have one," he said. He grabbed his cane. "Look after yourself. Call me every now and then, let me know how you're doing."

Jake watched Dean walk away, anger and shame and regret burning in the pit of his belly. Then Jake downed the last of his wine and walked slowly to his apartment, squinting against the last rays of the setting sun.

He dumped his bag and coat by the front door and went straight into the kitchen to grab a bottle of wine and a glass.

So, it was official—he was no longer a writer. Just another journalist. He walked to the living room and stared at the half a dozen copies of *The Coolabah Tree* on his bookcase. First editions, foreign translations, international editions. Jesus, he'd been so proud when he'd held his book in his hands for the first time. He and Marly had danced around the apartment and spilled champagne and gotten in trouble with the neighbors for making too much noise. He'd imagined half a dozen books filling the bookcase alongside his debut work.

Swearing, he crossed to his desk and powered up his computer. He pulled up a chair in front of a blank screen. He placed his fingers on the keyboard, his mind going over the story he'd outlined all those years ago, the story that was supposed to be the spine of his second novel.

Words formed in his mind, sentences. He began to type. But after a few minutes, his hands fell into his lap.

It wasn't right. Maybe he'd been out of the habit of writing fiction for so long, he'd forgotten how. Maybe the story was stale. Or maybe it really was over.

He stared at the screen.

I know you've got another book in you, Jake, but you need to give yourself permission to write it.

"What a load of bollocks."

Angry, he pushed away from the desk and reached for the wine bottle again. Dean could get stuffed. As for his amateur-hour theories about Marly and the baby... It was probably as well the old man wasn't representing him anymore.

7

A WEEK LATER, JAKE WAS making notes on an article in the café in the foyer of the *Herald* building when Macca and Jonesy pulled up chairs at the adjacent table. Jake exchanged a few words of greeting then returned to his work. He must have been listening to the other men's conversation on some level, however, because his ears pricked up when he heard Poppy's name. His pen stilled on the page but he didn't look up as he waited to hear more.

Macca had been mentoring Poppy since her first week on the job. In Jake's opinion, the other man was way too smitten to be objective. The way he followed Poppy around with his eyes was becoming the office joke.

"You're never going to know if you don't sling your hook, mate," Jonesy was saying, taking a huge bite out of a chicken schnitzel sandwich.

"There's no way she's single." Macca spoke with the resigned hopefulness of the truly besotted.

"Won't know till you ask. She's never mentioned anyone. Give it a go, see what she says."

Macca made a noncommittal noise.

"Up to you, buddy, but you're not the only one who wouldn't mind going for a bit of gold." Jonesy laughed at his own joke. "Saw Patrick from advertising sales doing the old smoothie routine on her the other day."

Jake frowned. Patrick Larson was a slick dickhead in an expensive suit. The thought of him smarming all over Poppy made Jake's neck itch.

"Matter of fact, if you're not going to make your move, I might just ask her out myself," Jonesy said.

Jake's head came up at that. Jonesy was leaning back in his chair, his belly pouring over his belt, crumbs from his lunch scattered over his shirtfront.

In your dreams, pal. Poppy is way too fine for you.

The flash of territorialism was disturbing. Poppy was nothing to him. They were barely on speaking terms, despite having cleared the air last week.

He must have been glaring because Jonesy glanced at him, offering a just-between-the-boys grin. Jake frowned and the other man's smile faded.

"Anyway. Better get back to it," Jonesy said, standing and brushing debris from his shirt.

Jake sat staring at his notes after they'd left. Someone should say something to Poppy. Warn her. Because it was obvious what was going to happen—Macca would ask her out. Or Patrick. Or—God forbid—Jonesy. And before she knew it, guys would be nudging each other all over the building. It wasn't only male athletes a female reporter had to worry about in this profession. Like it or not, journalism was still a boys' club.

He grabbed his notes and crossed to the elevator. As he exited on the fifth floor, he saw Poppy shuffling papers together near the printer and diverted from his course to his desk to stop in front of her.

"Got a minute?" he asked.

She flicked a look at him. He'd never noticed before, but she had very long lashes. So long that they swept her cheekbones when she glanced down at the papers in her hands.

"It depends," she said.

"What on?"

"What it's about."

"Right." He'd walked into that one. "It's, uh, private."

One of her eyebrows rose. "Please don't tell me you've got a nasty rash."

It was so unexpected he laughed. He'd forgotten how dry she could be. How fast on her feet.

"No rash. Everything's in tip-top working order," he said.

"So did you just want to give me a status report or was there something else?" she asked.

"It's about Macca."

"Right."

"And Jonesy. And that Patrick dickhead from sales."

"He's not a dickhead. He was very helpful when I was looking for some information the other day."

Jake stabbed a finger at her. "Exactly. He wants to get you into bed. Along with Macca and Jonesy."

"You mean like a...a foursome?" she asked, incredulous.

She looked so appalled he had to laugh.

"No. Separately. Every man for himself."

"Right. Very funny." She shook her head and turned to walk away.

He grabbed her arm. "Don't you believe me?"

She gave him a withering look. "I'm not an idiot. Despite recent behavior that might indicate otherwise."

She glanced pointedly at his fingers circling her arm, but he didn't let go. Partly because he hadn't finished talking to her, and partly because she felt good and it had been too long since he'd touched her.

"Trust me. Macca has a crush on you. And Patrick collects scalps like baseball cards. As for Jonesy...well, he's not blind."

She shook her head again. She had no idea how attractive she was. Tall and strong and supple. Curvy in all the right places, with a pretty, open face that hinted at an enjoyment of the simple things in life. Like food and wine and sex.

"Why are we even having this conversation, Stevens?"

She'd started calling him by his last name since their road trip. He didn't like it. He'd been inside her. He'd pressed his face into the soft, silken skin of her inner thighs. He'd made her purr with pleasure. He figured at the very least that put them on a first-name basis.

"A while back you asked me to step in if I thought you were putting a foot wrong. One pro to another," he said.

"And?"

"I just wanted to warn you that sleeping with one of the guys from the department would definitely fall under that category."

She stared at him. She opened her mouth, closed it, then shook her head. "Are you *seriously* warning me against screwing one of my coworkers?"

"You asked me to give you a heads-up if you needed it."

She huffed out a laugh, but he didn't think she was amused. More incredulous, if he didn't miss his guess.

"Unbelievable," she muttered under her breath. Then she turned away from him.

"Hang on a minute." She had no idea how gossipy a bunch of guys could get over a few beers. He grabbed her arm again.

"Do you mind?" she said coolly.

"I don't think you're taking this very seriously," he said.

She stared at him. They were standing so close he could see her nostrils flare. He could smell her deodorant and whatever soap she washed her clothes in, could feel the warmth of her body.

"Do you honestly think I need another lesson on why screwing someone I work with is a sucky idea, Stevens? Really?"

For a moment he saw clear through to her soul, saw the regret and the embarrassment she felt over their few sweaty, hot encounters.

She wished it had never happened. It was there as plain as day in her eyes. If she could, she'd wind back the clock and reclaim the hours they'd lost in each other's arms. Even though it had been the best sex he'd ever had. Even though he couldn't stop thinking about it, about her, she wished it out of existence.

He let her go. She strode to her desk. He crossed to his own desk and dumped his jacket and notes. His wine club order had been delivered while he was at lunch and he shoved the carton to one side as he sat and called up his e-mail in-box. Then he stared at it unseeingly.

He didn't regret sleeping with her. Not for a second. Even though it had made things weird at work. It had been worth it—that was how good it had been.

But to Poppy, he was just some guy she worked with who she'd slipped up with on the road. She'd filed him under the same heading as Macca and Patrick and Jonesy. Despite the many moan-inducing orgasms he'd given her. Despite the fact that he'd left George, her battery-operated friend, for dead. Despite the laughter they'd shared and the challenge of their conversations.

It was a humbling realization. And an uncomfortable one.

You should be thanking your lucky stars. She could be crying all over the place, blabbing to the other women on the floor. You could be getting dirty looks from everyone with two X chromosomes within a one-mile radius.

He didn't feel grateful, however. He felt pissed. Dissatisfied. Frustrated.

A phone rang across the office and he came out of his daze. He reached for his mouse. What was it Poppy had said to him last week?

Get over yourself.

Maybe she had a point. He had no right demanding anything from her, including recognition that what had happened between them had been out of the ordinary. Not when he had nothing to offer in exchange. He wasn't looking to start something up with someone. Not now, not ever.

He concentrated on proofing his article with new resolve. So what if he was too aware of everything Poppy said or did, every move she made? So what if he only had to think of touching her breasts, sliding his hand between her legs and he had a hard-on that wouldn't quit? It didn't matter. It meant nothing. It was over.

THE NOTICING-POPPY'S-every-move thing came back to haunt Jake later that evening as he worked at his desk. Slowly the department emptied until only the hard-core workaholics were left. Which meant it was down to him and Poppy, essentially. He was aware of her crossing back and forth between the printer and her desk, then going in to talk to Leonard before hitting her computer again. Leonard left at seven, but Poppy remained at her desk. He glanced at her as he headed for the kitchen to forage for something to keep him going for a few more hours. She was kneading her forehead as she frowned at a page, red pen in hand. The page was covered in little notes to herself, lines and arrows, deletions and insertions. Tension radiated from her in palpable waves.

He poured himself a tall glass of water in the kitchen and unearthed a stash of muesli bars someone thought they'd hidden at the back of the cupboard. He grabbed one for himself, then went back for a second. He dropped it on her desk as he walked past.

"Can't think without food," he said over his shoulder.

She didn't say a word, but he heard the rustle as she tore open the package. She was still working away with the red pen when he shrugged into his jacket and picked up the carton of wine. He hovered for a beat, watching her. She looked tired, but he knew there was no way she was leaving her desk until she was satisfied.

She'd probably tell him to take a long walk off a short pier, but he couldn't help himself. Which was becoming a bit of a recurring theme where she was concerned. Couldn't stop himself from poking her with a stick. Couldn't stop himself from wanting her. Couldn't stop himself from having her. Couldn't stop himself from feeling for her.

She slid the printout she was working on under today's edition of the paper when he stopped beside her desk. She sat back in her chair and looked up at him, one eyebrow raised.

"What?" she asked as though he was a pesky kid annoying her in the playground.

"You want some help?"

Her expression immediately became guarded. "I'm fine."

"Yeah? How late were you planning on working? How many red pens you planning on running through?"

Her mouth tightened. "I'll work it out."

"Anyone ever told you you're stubborn?"

Before she could react, he snatched her article out from beneath the newspaper.

"Hey!" She was on her feet in a second, trying to grab the paper from his hands.

He held it out high from his side. If she wanted to get it she was going to have to wrestle him for it. She seemed to be considering doing just that for a moment, then her shoulders slumped.

"Fine, I'm sure you could do with a good laugh after a long day."

He frowned at her defeated posture and lowered his hand so he could read what she'd written. The page was so crossed and marked with red it was almost impossible to decipher the original text.

"Move over," he said, nudging her to one side.

Without asking, he took her seat and used the mouse to take him back to the top of her article on the computer screen. He could feel her nervousness as she hovered behind him while he read. It took him thirty seconds to see where the problem lay.

"This isn't as bad as you think it is," he said.

"Thanks," she said drily.

He shot her a look. "Pull up a chair."

She eyed him for a long moment, then slowly pulled over the chair from a nearby desk.

He pointed to the screen.

"You're overthinking this too much, overwriting. It's an interview. People will read it because it's about David Hannam and he's the country's number one tennis star, not because you're being clever. You just need to feed them some of what they expect, then throw in a few little surprises. Make them feel they've found out something they didn't know before."

"Easy for you to say."

He could hear the tiredness in her voice. She was running on empty.

"What's the most interesting thing he said to you when you interviewed him?" he asked suddenly.

She blinked, then frowned.

"No, don't think about it—just say the first thing that comes into your head."

"Okay. When he was a kid, he wanted to be an astronaut. He didn't discover tennis until he was fifteen."

"Great. There's your opener."

He rolled his chair to one side and gestured for her to take his place at the keyboard. She did so slowly, warily.

He watched as she placed her fingers on the keys. Then she sighed and let them drop into her lap.

"I can't do this with you watching."

"Yeah, you can. They're just words, Poppy. Words and ideas."

"Not by the time I'm finished with them," she said ruefully.

"Pretend you're having a beer with some mates and telling them about the interview. You're not going to bother with any of the boring crap up front. Who cares what his stats are? Bury that stuff toward the end for the nerds. Tell a story."

She put her fingers to the keyboard again and started writing.

When David Hannam was a kid, he wanted to be an astronaut. He figured that flying through space and looking at the earth would be about the coolest thing ever. Of course, that was before he discovered the thrill of standing in a packed stadium with the winner's trophy in his hands...

She wrote for twenty minutes, stopping and starting. Every time she went to press the delete key he caught her hand.

"Just write what comes to you. You can edit later."

Finally she stopped typing.

"Good. Now cut and paste this paragraph. And this one. And those two," he said, pointing out the material from her previous draft.

He sat beside her for another hour as she finalized the interview. Finally she hit the key to send it to the subeditor for tomorrow's edition.

She let out a sigh, then scrubbed her face with her hands.

"Thank you," she said.

"It was no big deal."

"To you, maybe. This stuff is second nature to you."

"I've been doing it for fifteen years, Poppy."

She shrugged. She was a perfectionist, that was her problem. And she was used to being the best.

"If it makes you feel any better, I can't dive worth shit. And my backstroke is laughable."

She gave him a dry look.

"It's true." He stood and grabbed her elbow to encourage her to stand, also. He passed her her jacket.

"Go home. Eat. Sleep. Stop thinking."

"Easy for you to say," she said for the second time that night.

He laughed. "You think I don't think?"

"I have my doubts sometimes. Like this afternoon when you warned me not to screw the crew." She was smiling. He felt an absurd sense of achievement.

"I was protecting your honor."

"Is that what you call it? I thought you were pissing in the corners."

Startled, he looked at her face. She cocked an eyebrow at him and he realized she was right—he *had* been pissing in the corners, marking his territory. Making sure she didn't hook up with one of the other guys from work.

"Well, I never said *I* was honorable," he said.

They walked toward the elevator. The cleaners had come and gone and the lights were dim, only the glow from various computers and electrical devices and the occasional desk

lamp illuminating the newsroom. He stood to one side to let
Poppy enter the elevator before him. He didn't mean to, but
somehow his eyes sought out the shadowy V at the neckline
of her shirt as she moved past him. He could see a thin line
of black lace and his mind filled with images of Poppy's full,
creamy breasts spilling out of black satin.

He reined in his libido in time to note that she hit the button
for the foyer rather than the basement parking garage. There
was only one reason for her to be getting out at ground level—
she planned to walk across to Flinders Street station and catch
the train home.

"Car still in the shop?" he guessed.

She gave him a startled look. "How did you—"

"I'm a journalist. We notice things."

"Right."

"You want a lift?"

Given the black lace fantasy that he'd just beaten back
with a stick, it wasn't such a smart idea. But he had a long
track record of not being smart around Poppy.

"It's out of your way."

"You don't know that. Where do you live?"

"Malvern. Miles away from South Yarra."

She kept her eyes on the floor indicator but a small frown
appeared between her eyebrows. He smiled. Poppy had
looked up his home address. Interesting.

"I'll drive you. Might as well—I've got the car tonight,
since I knew this was coming." He indicated the carton of
wine in his arms.

"I'll be fine."

"It's past nine, Poppy. Don't be stupid."

"That's why I'm saying no—I'm not being stupid."

She met his eyes then and he knew that she'd noticed him

looking at her breasts. She was probably aware that he was half-hard, too, in the same way that he was aware that she was breathing a little too quickly and her pupils had dilated with desire.

"It's just a lift home."

He wasn't sure if that was a lie or not. All he knew was that he wanted to spend more time with her.

She looked at the floor. The lift pinged open at the foyer level. She didn't move. He reached out and hit the door closed button.

"Nothing is going to happen," she said.

"I know."

But he was fully hard now, every inch of him craving her. He wanted to duck his head and inhale the scent from the nape of her neck. He wanted to slide his hands beneath her shirt and cup her breasts. He wanted to watch her face as she moaned and pleaded and came.

He couldn't sleep with her again. Not after the conversation they'd had last week where she'd more or less confirmed that she wasn't the kind of woman who did casual sex.

It was a pity his body hadn't gotten the memo yet. Forcing his mind to thoughts of frolicking puppies and old ladies with canes, he led Poppy to his car.

POPPY SLID INTO THE SMOOTH embrace of butter-soft leather upholstery and reached for her seat belt.

Was she *nuts?* What on earth was she doing letting Jake Stevens drive her home?

And how had she not noticed last time she'd been in his car that he drove a Porsche? She'd been so numb she'd barely registered the color, let alone the make, but now she was fully aware that he drove the kind of sleek and sexy car that screamed sex and power and lots of other things that weren't doing anything to slow the pulse beating low in her belly.

You idiot.

Self-abuse wasn't going to help, either. She'd been a goner the moment Jake had stopped beside her desk and leaned close enough for her to smell the unique scent that was aftershave, soap, laundry detergent and hot male skin. Heady at the best of times, but absolutely deadly when her dreams had been haunted by long, liquid moments from her two nights with Jake.

She wasn't sure what it said for her psyche that even though she wasn't sure she liked him much, she still craved his body.

She winced and stared out the passenger side window. Who was she kidding? She liked him. She liked him plenty. She thought he was funny and clever. And he'd proven himself to be kind, in action if not in word. Just because he wasn't interested in having a relationship with her didn't negate any of that. Even if he had embarrassed her and made her feel gauche and foolish with his midnight flight. And even if he'd had the outrageous gall to point out to her that sleeping with a work colleague was a dumb idea—as though she hadn't worked that one out about five seconds after discovering the other side of the bed was empty.

At the end of the day, he'd never promised her anything. And she was aware that her grief and upset over Uncle Charlie probably didn't put her in the best position to judge this situation rationally. But she was also aware that only a very, very foolish and self-destructive person would put her head in the lion's mouth twice. Especially when said person had a weakness for said lion, and said lion was licking his chops and had a speculative gleam in his eye.

"Whereabouts in Malvern are you?" he asked. He held up a hand. "Wait, let me guess. Near the pool, right?"

She hated giving him the satisfaction of being right, but he was.

"Yes. How did you know?" she asked, irony heavy in her tone.

"I'm a journalist. We—"

"Notice things. Thank you, I got that the first time."

He was grinning, and the corners of her own mouth were curling upward.

"Do you still swim?"

"Every day." She felt a little stupid admitting it. She was retired, after all. She was supposed to be getting a life outside of the pool. But ever since losing Uncle Charlie, she'd craved the comfort of the familiar and she'd given in to the urge to swim every day, either before or after work.

"Not today, though, right?" he asked. "Surely even you aren't going to do laps after nine at night?"

"The pool is closed," she said. "Plus I swam this morning."

"Better be careful, Birmingham. You're gonna lose that spectacular rack if you keep training so hard."

She shot him a startled look. His attention was on the road but he was grinning hugely.

"I think the less attention you pay to my rack the better."

"Wise words. Would you consider wearing a burlap bag as your part of the bargain?"

She laughed. As always with him, she couldn't help it. He was just so damned cocky and incorrigible. If someone had asked her beforehand if such a combination would appeal to her, she would have laughed in their face. Which went to show how well she knew herself.

Another disturbing thought.

"Do you have these kinds of conversations with Hilary or Mary? Because it's not going to be long before you're up on sexual harassment charges if you do."

"I haven't slept with Hilary or Mary," he said.

"Very restrained of you."

"I've never slept with anyone from the paper before."

He was still watching the road. She eyed his profile for a long moment.

"Wow. I guess I should feel flattered."

He smiled faintly. "But you don't?"

"It was a stupid thing to do."

"Maybe."

She frowned, wondering what he meant by that. There was no doubt in her mind that she'd screwed up monumentally when she'd let him lay hands on her. Amazing orgasms aside.

The sustained gurgle of her hungry stomach cut through the silence in the car. She pressed a hand to her belly.

"Sorry."

"I'm starving, too. Maybe we should stop for a burger. There's a drive-through on High Street, isn't there?"

She made a face. "Plastic food. Disgusting."

"Says Ms. Chocolate Chip and Nacho Cheese."

She blinked. He remembered what she'd had in her shopping bag up in Queensland. Either he had an amazing memory, or… She didn't allow herself to complete the thought. No doubt, if she questioned him under bright lights, he'd tell her he was a journalist, and he noticed things.

"At least it's made from real cream and real sugar and real fat," she said. "Haven't you seen that documentary about fast food?"

"No. Why on earth would I voluntarily rule out one of the major food groups from my diet by learning a bunch of stuff that would make it impossible for me to ever eat it again?"

She shook her head. "So bad for you."

"Lots of things are. Doesn't stop most of us from indulging."

There was something about the way he said *indulging* that made her want to squirm in her seat. Damn him. Only Jake Stevens could make a single word sound so…provocative.

"There's an Indian takeout a little farther up. If you must eat crap."

"I must. And so must you. I have it on good authority that your body requires sustenance."

She was about to argue but her stomach growled again.

"See?"

She rolled her eyes but still ordered chicken tikka masala, vegetable korma and a plain naan bread when they stopped at the Indian restaurant. Ten minutes later they were back in Jake's car, the heady smell of spicy food rising around them. She directed him to her street and he stopped outside her apartment block. She opened the car door before she turned to thank him.

"I appreciate the lift. I know it was out of your way."

"Not a problem," he said.

His face was cast in shadows, but she could see the gleam of his eyes in the soft light from the dash. She felt a ridiculous impulse to lean forward and press a kiss to the angle of his jaw. Just to see if he felt and tasted as good as she remembered.

Hunger was clearly making her light-headed. She swung her legs out of the car and stood.

"Anyway. See you tomorrow," she said. Then she remembered it was Friday. "I mean, Monday," she quickly amended.

"Have a good weekend, Poppy."

She pushed the car door closed and turned away, but she couldn't help thinking that he was a good fifteen minutes from home and by the time he got there his naan bread would be more soggy than light and fluffy and his samosas more spongy than crunchy. Before she could edit herself, she turned on her heel and rapped on the side window of his car.

The glass lowered with a discreet hum and Jake looked out at her, eyebrows raised questioningly. She studied his mouth before she spoke. If there was even a hint of that knowing, smug smile of his… But he wasn't smiling. He was watching her, his expression unreadable.

She swallowed a sudden lump of nervousness.

"If you want to come up and eat your food before it gets cold, that would be okay."

As invitations went, it wasn't the most gracious she'd ever issued. But maybe that was for the best. Maybe her awkwardness would make him say no and she could put this moment of madness behind her.

"That would be great. If you don't mind."

"Of course not."

They sounded like two scrupulously polite old ladies. She waited for him to exit his car and lock it. Then she led him upstairs to her second-floor apartment. Her gaze immediately went to the stack of newspapers piled on the dining room table, then to the tower of dirty cereal bowls on the kitchen counter, then to the basket full of laundry on her armchair. If she'd known she'd be entertaining guests, she'd have cleaned up a little this morning instead of gulping down her breakfast and racing for the bus.

"Um, sorry about the mess," she said. She dumped her bag of food on the counter and began clearing up.

"Relax. I'm not about to whip out my white gloves. My place is a pigsty."

"Really?"

"Hell, yeah. Who has time to clean? I thought about hiring someone to come in once a week, but it seems pretty shameful when I live in a two-bedroom apartment."

"Ditto." She forced herself to relax and dumped the cereal bowls in the sink instead of stacking them in the dishwasher. She pulled out two plates and some cutlery, then gestured for him to take a seat at the table. "Your food's getting cold."

He sat at the end of the table and she sat on one of the sides, facing the window. For a moment there was only the rustle of plastic bags and the snap of containers being opened as they loaded up their plates.

She stole a glance at him as she tore off a chunk of her naan bread. Jake Stevens, in her apartment. She couldn't quite believe it. After the way he'd treated her when she first started at the paper, then the way she'd felt when he'd pulled his midnight disappearing act... Well, she hadn't exactly anticipated this moment.

"You own this place or rent?" Jake asked as he dipped one of his samosas into yogurt sauce.

"Own. Uncle Charlie insisted I do something sensible when I started getting sponsorship money."

"Smart man."

"Yeah. What about you? Own or rent?"

Good grief. Could this conversation be any more stilted?

Jake smiled at her as though he could hear her thoughts.

"Own. Same deal—I decided to do something a little more long-term than buy a hot car when *The Coolabah Tree* was a surprise success."

"Then you went ahead and bought the car anyway."

"I'm only human. I believe Tom Cruise said it best in *Risky Business*—'Porsche. There is no substitute.'"

"Wow. You sure know your Tom Cruise. I'm...disturbed. Which is your favorite scene in *Top Gun?* The topless volleyball game or the topless shower scene?"

He grinned and scooped up a spoonful of rice. "And you think I'm a smart-ass."

She smiled down at her plate. She liked sparring with

him. A little more than was healthy, if she was being honest with herself.

His gaze wandered to the pile of newspapers. He frowned slightly, then tugged the top paper toward himself. It was opened to the sports section and she realized too late what he was looking at—the notes she'd made in the margin when she read his article this morning. She'd gotten into the habit of analyzing his writing, trying to deconstruct it so she could pick up some clues for her own work.

She leaned across the table, ready to snatch it from his hands. Jake threw her a curious look and she retreated to her chair.

"It's nothing. Just some notes for school," she said.

"School?"

"I'm taking a journalism course at night school."

She waited for him to say something mocking but he didn't. He simply returned his attention to the newspaper and her penciled-in notes. She tried to remember what she'd written.

Please, nothing about how much I admire his writing. Anything but that.

"You enjoying it?" he asked after a long moment. He put the paper down and slid it away from himself.

"Um, school, you mean?" she asked, her attention on the newspaper. She desperately wanted to grab it and check that she hadn't written anything too revealing, but she knew that would only make her look even more foolish.

"School, the paper. The whole thing."

"Sure. It's a challenge, but that's only because it's new. And I feel like I'm slowly starting to find my feet."

Okay, that was a lie, but she wasn't about to admit the truth.

He nodded, using his bread to wipe sauce off his plate. "You were right—this is good stuff. Much better than a burger."

She watched as he licked a smudge of sauce off his bottom

lip. Between anxiety about what he might have read in the margins of the paper and her hyperawareness of him physically, her appetite had completely deserted her. She pushed her half-finished plate away and used a paper napkin to wipe her own mouth.

"You don't do anything by halves, do you?" Jake asked suddenly. Her startled gaze found his. They stared at each other for a long moment.

"No. Sometimes I wish I could. But I can't. It's just the way I'm built."

He reached across and caught her hand in his. His thumb stroked the back of hers as he cradled her palm.

"You have beautiful eyes, Poppy Birmingham, you know that? Someone should have written about them when they were mentioning all those gold medals you won."

She forgot to breathe for a moment. His hand slipped from hers and he pushed back his chair. He started shoving empty take-out containers into one of the bags.

She felt very uncertain all of a sudden. She didn't understand him. Every now and then she thought she had a reading on him, but he kept taking her by surprise.

"Leave it. I have to clean in the morning, anyway."

"Do you mind if I use your bathroom before I go?" he asked. She nodded. "Down the hall, to the right."

He'd have to pass her bedroom on the way. She resigned herself to the fact that he'd see her wildly messed bed, the clothes strewn everywhere, her underwear kicked into the corner, the books piled beside her bed. So much for keeping her distance from him. By the time he left her apartment there wouldn't be a single one of her shortcomings and foibles he wouldn't be aware of.

Which reminded her…

She grabbed the newspaper he'd abandoned and reviewed her notes. She'd underlined a couple of phrases, passages that had really appealed to her. Nothing too incriminating— except for the two words she'd scribbled in the margin: *talented bastard.*

Great. Now he knew she admired him professionally, as well as desired him personally.

She heard footsteps in the hallway and hastily dropped the newspaper onto the table. She tried to look casual and at ease, but her shoulders felt as though they were up around her earlobes.

Jake was holding something in his hand when he entered. It took her a moment to recognize the copy of his book that she'd exiled to the toilet-paper basket.

She closed her eyes. This evening was getting better and better.

"I'm curious. If I look through this, are there going to be any pages missing?"

"Oh. Um. No. Of course not. I'm not even sure what that was doing in the bathroom…."

Jake cocked his head to one side and the lie died in her throat.

They stared at each other, then his mouth stretched into a grin.

"Just how long have I been gracing the smallest room in the house, anyway?"

"Since my first day on the paper." He'd surprised her again. His writing was not something she'd expected him to have a sense of humor about.

"That long. Did it make you feel better, putting me in there?" he asked, weighing the book in his hand.

"Yes."

"Good."

He turned to leave the room and she realized he was going to put the book back where he'd found it.

"No. Don't," she said. "I don't think I want it in there any-more."

He stilled. "It's not a bad place for it."

"Maybe."

Jake turned to face her. Their eyes met across the space that separated them, and suddenly they were at the point they'd both been dancing around all night. Poppy could feel her heart kicking in her chest, feel the flood of adrenaline racing through her body. Deep inside, her body throbbed in anticipation.

She wanted him. And she knew he wanted her. Could practically smell it in the air.

"Where do you want it, then?" he asked.

"I used to keep it in my bedroom."

His eyes darkened. "I don't think that's the best place for it."

"Why not?" She held her breath, waiting for his answer. They both knew they weren't talking about his book or her apartment.

"Because it's your space. It's too personal," he said quietly.

So.

She nodded to let him know she understood his message. She hoped her disappointment didn't show on her face. Maybe this time she'd learn her lesson where he was concerned.

She held her hand out for the book.

"Okay. I guess I'll have to find a new home for it. Some-where between the toilet and the bedroom."

He passed the book over. They both turned toward the hall. She moved ahead of him to open the front door. She kept her hand on the lock, gripping the cool metal tightly as he hesi-tated in the doorway.

"It's not you, Poppy. I really like you."

She shrugged. "I get it. We work with each other. Things have already been awkward. I get it."

"It's not about work." He ran a hand through his hair, stared at the floor for a long beat. "I don't want to hurt you."

"Then don't," she said simply.

He lifted his head to meet her eyes. "It's not that simple."

"Yeah, it is. I'm not asking for a marriage proposal, Jake. I just want you to be there when I wake in the morning. Or to at least say goodbye before you go."

He searched her face. She could feel the tension in him. "I don't have anything to offer you."

Right now she was focused on only one thing—the rush of blood in her ears, the spread of warmth in the pit of her stomach.

"Can you be here in the morning?" she asked. "That's all I want from you right now."

He closed his eyes. "Do you have any idea how much I've thought about you over the past few weeks?" His voice was rough and low. It scraped along her senses and sent a shiver through her.

"It's not like I've been counting sheep at night, either."

His eyes opened. "What have you been counting, then?"

She smiled slowly. "What do you think?"

By slow degrees his smile grew to match hers. He took a step forward and she met him halfway. The press of her breasts against his chest was almost a relief.

His eyes glinted as he lowered his head toward hers. She opened her mouth to him and closed her eyes as his tongue swept into her mouth. He sipped at her lips, stroked her tongue with his, murmured something deep in his throat. She let go of the door and reached for his hips, pulling him closer. He was already hard, his erection straining the fine cord of his pants. She slid a hand onto his butt and held him against her, savoring the heat and hardness of him.

After a long moment he lifted his head. She stared into his face, drugged with need.

"Yes. The answer is yes. I can be here in the morning," he said

Just as well, because she wasn't sure she had the willpower to push him away if his answer had been anything different.

"Then what are you waiting for?"

Taking his hand, she shut the door behind them and led him to her bedroom.

8

POPPY'S ROOM LOOKED AS THOUGH a bomb had hit it. Clothes and shoes everywhere, books stacked beside the bed, her chest of drawers strewn with papers and toiletries. About the only space that was clear was the bed. Which was good, since that was Jake's destination.

"Sorry about the mess," she said.

Jake grunted to let her know he didn't give a damn about the cleanliness or otherwise of her bedroom and pulled her down onto the mattress, eager to feel the warmth of her beneath him. Every night she'd slipped into his dreams, taunting him with remembered passion. He wasn't sure where he wanted to touch first, which part of her he needed to taste the most. He tugged at her clothes, yanking off her jacket then fumbling with her shirt.

"Slow down." She laughed.

"Can't."

And it was true, he couldn't. He'd been convinced he'd never slide his hands over her breasts again, and yet here they were, warm and full and soft in his hands, her nipples hard beneath the silk and lace of her bra. He'd been certain he'd never feel the greedy press of her hips against his again, or the firm strength of her long legs tangling with his. And yet she was even now rubbing herself against him, one leg wrapped around his waist as she sought satisfaction.

It was too much. She was too much. He sucked a nipple, lace and all, into his mouth, laving her with his tongue. She moaned and he slid a hand down her belly and into the waist band of her tailored pants. The button gave way easily, the zipper hissed down, then he was sliding his hand over the plumpness of her mound, his fingers gliding into damp curls then into hot, slick flesh. He slid a finger inside her, felt the instinctive tightening of her muscles as she clenched them around him. She was so hot, so tight. He wanted to be there, needed to be there. He pushed her trousers down, as clumsy and urgent as a schoolboy. She laughed, the sound low and sultry, as he freed himself from his pants. A moment to protect them both, then he was inside her, his pace already wild, his whole body taut with need.

No laughter from her then, just a dreamy, distant look in her eyes as she bit her lip and tilted her head back and thrust her hips in rhythm with his.

He ducked his head to her breasts again, using his teeth to pull the silk of her bra cup down so he could bite her dusky nipple before tugging it into his mouth. Her hips bucked be-neath him as he flicked his tongue over and over her. He slid his hands beneath her hips and drove himself to the hilt again and again. She felt so good. Everything about her. Her skin. The softness of her breasts. The plumpness of her mound. The slick tightness between her thighs.

"Poppy," he whispered against her skin.

"I know," she whispered.

Then he was coming, his climax squeezing his chest, his belly, his thighs. He ground himself against her, feeling her own climax pulse around him. For long seconds he remained tautly above her and inside her. And then he collapsed on top of her, his breath coming in choppy gasps.

"Pinch me," she said after a short while.

"Is this a kinky thing or…?"

"I just want to make sure this is real."

He lifted his head to look into her face. Man, he loved the slightly bewildered look she got on her face after he'd made her come. As though she wasn't one hundred percent certain which way was up or down.

He withdrew from her and rolled to the edge of the bed.

"Come on," he said, reaching for her hand. "Let's have a shower. I couldn't help noticing you have this handy bench tiled into the wall in there."

"For when I was training, to help loosen me up. Back when we weren't on water restrictions because of the drought."

"Ah, the good old days," he said. His trousers and boxer briefs were still tangled around his ankles and he kicked them off. He tugged her pants the rest of the way off, too, then ran a hand from her knee up her thigh, over her hip, stopping on the flat plane of her belly. He felt her muscles contract beneath his hand, watched as her nipples hardened all over again. Her lips parted and she watched him through half-lowered lids.

"Come have a shower," he said.

"Okay."

She led the way up the short hallway. He watched the sway of her hips, the tight flex of her butt. He couldn't resist sliding his hands onto it, cupping it in his palms.

"Just out of curiosity, you ever tried to crack a walnut with these suckers?" he asked, squeezing the twin cheeks of her derriere firmly.

She gave him a look over her shoulder. He grinned and shrugged.

"Just curious."

"Hmm," she said. "I'm not sure I want to know what other questions you have floating in that brain of yours."

He stood back and watched some more as she reached to turn on the shower. Even in winter she had a light tan from her hours in the pool. He eyed the lines on her ass from her swimsuit and remembered how creamy and smooth her breasts were in comparison with her golden arms and legs.

He was hard again. More than anything he wanted to press her against the shower wall and slide inside her again, but there were other, more pressing issues to attend to. Like the fact that he'd been craving another taste of her for weeks now.

"You coming?" she asked as she stepped beneath the water.

He smiled and stepped in after her. "Definitely."

He reached for the soap and the washcloth hanging from her shower organizer. She watched as he worked up a good lather on the cloth.

"Now," he said, drawing her toward him. Slowly he washed her from head to toe. He traced the whorls of her ears, mapped the elegance of her long neck. Paid loving, intimate attention to her breasts and her armpits and the curve of her hip. Dipped between her thighs, washed behind her knees. Then he knelt and lifted her feet, one by one, and washed her toes and her soles and her heels, his fingers massaging the washcloth against her skin.

When he was finished, he looked up at her.

"Sit down," he said.

Poppy's eyes widened as she guessed his intention. Then her focus dropped to his erection where it pressed, hard and ready, against his belly.

"I want—"

"Later."

She sat on the tiled bench behind her. He moved between

her legs, pushing them apart. The air was thick with steam and moisture and warm water pounded down on both of them. He parted the pinkness of her folds. She sucked in an anticipatory breath. He glanced up at her, taking in the flush on her cheeks, the heaviness of her eyelids.

Then he lowered his head and tasted her.

Better than he'd remembered. Slick, silky flesh, the gentle musk of her sex, the freshness of her arousal. He used his hands to keep her open, circling his thumbs around and around her entrance as he teased her clitoris with his mouth. She was very turned on, the bud stiff against his tongue and he sucked her into his mouth again and again. Her hips bucked and one of her hands slid into his hair and fisted there. She lifted a leg to brace it on the seat beside her, offering him greater access. He slid a finger inside her and stroked her inner walls. He knew the moment he found the spot he was looking for—her whole body tensed as though she'd been shocked.

"Jake," she panted.

He smiled against her sex and renewed his assault, stroking her clitoris with his tongue, stroking her G-spot with his finger. It didn't take long. She sucked in a deep breath, her hips lifting. He clamped a hand onto her thigh to hold her in place. He stayed with her as her body convulsed with pleasure, her inner muscles vibrating around his finger.

He lifted his head at last and looked up at her, savoring the abandoned, provocative picture she made, her head dropped back against the shower wall, water streaming down her peaked breasts and her flat belly.

He'd meant to wait, to dry her and take her to bed, but he couldn't hold off a second longer. Standing, he took himself in hand and nudged her folds with his erection.

"Yes," she said, lifting her hips.

He was inside her, gritting his teeth at how wet she was, how good she felt. She shuddered, a whole body ripple of need.

He withdrew until just the tip of his cock remained inside her then watched as he pressed forward and his cock disappeared into her body once more. He repeated the move, reveling in the greedy clutch of her body, savoring the glide into tightness as he drove into her. He glanced at her face, saw she was watching the place where they were joined, too, and that her breasts were rising and falling rapidly. They locked gazes and suddenly he was on the verge, just like that, pleasure rushing through his body. Swiftly, he withdrew from her, stroking himself once, twice with his hand until he came on her belly, his body shuddering.

"I think maybe I just died," she said.

He laughed. He'd never met a woman so open about her own pleasure. With Poppy there had never been any games, no pretense that she didn't want him, that she didn't enjoy the sex, that it wasn't important to her.

She was equally honest about her feelings, too. Another thing he found attractive. He couldn't ever imagine Poppy sulking or punishing him with silence. If she wanted something, she either asked for it or dealt with her need in some other way.

They made love again when they returned to the bedroom. He honestly hadn't thought he was up to it—he wasn't a perpetually horny teenager anymore—but watching her crawl on all fours to the far side of the mattress had his cock flooding to life again. He slid into her from behind this time while they both lay on their sides, her backside cradled by his hips. They rocked together for long, lazy minutes until desire took over. Then Poppy moved onto her hands and knees and he slammed himself into her until they both came yet again.

Poppy dragged the quilt up over their bodies afterward,

shaking her head and laughing ruefully when he slid a hand onto her breast.

"Give me five minutes," she said.

They fell asleep, his hand on her breast, his body curved against hers. His thoughts drifted to the way they fit as he slipped into sleep. She was so tall, he felt all of her against all of him. A good feeling. Complete.

JAKE WOKE WITH SUNLIGHT warm against his face. He turned his head, and there Poppy was, golden light streaming in her bedroom window, gilding her breasts. She was awake, too, her hair was mussed, her eyes heavy.

She smiled faintly when she caught his eye. "You're here."

"Yep."

"A minor miracle."

He smoothed the sole of his foot down the side of her smooth calf. "Hardly." He held her gaze when he said it, wanting her to know that if it was only about her, her honesty and funniness and desirability, he would never have left her bed. Her gaze slid away, but her smile remained.

She didn't know where she stood with him. Which was fair enough—he had no idea where he stood, either.

"There's cereal and bread if you're hungry, but I usually have breakfast at the pool on the weekends. There's a cute little café, and they make great pancakes." She said the words carefully, not quite issuing an invitation.

"Does a person have to swim laps to qualify for breakfast? Or can a person just sit back like a fat bastard and watch other people exercise?"

Her eyebrows rose, then a smile spread across her face. She tried to get it under control, to tame it, but he could still see her pleasure in her eyes even after she'd reined in her mouth

A moment of doubt bit him. She was so damned open, the way she broadcast everything via her big gray eyes and her expressive face.

He didn't want to hurt her. He remembered what she'd said last night—*then don't*. She'd been asking him to be honest with her. To commit to a night. To one moment at a time.

Could it really be that easy?

Poppy made him walk the two blocks to the pool, claiming it was a good warm-up. The sky was a pale blue, but the sun was shining. The Harold Holt Memorial Pool had two offerings for patrons to choose from: a smaller, heated indoor pool and a competition-length beast outside. The indoor pool was frothing with bodies, since it was September and the tail end of winter was still in the air outside. Only the serious swimmers were prepared to brave the elements for a more challenging swim. Predictably, Poppy led him outside.

She shucked her tracksuit pants immediately and started swinging her arms in broad circles. He frowned and eyed the swimmers churning up the lanes.

"Come on, scaredy cat," she said.

She'd talked him into borrowing a pair of board shorts a "friend" had left behind in her apartment, promising him that while he could still have his pancake breakfast without doing some laps, it would be that much more delicious once he'd earned it.

He'd always been skeptical of that argument—he'd enjoyed plenty of things in his lifetime that he hadn't strictly earned. But he could see she wanted him to swim with her. And it seemed like a small, simple sacrifice to make to bring that slow smile to her lips again.

"I wasn't joking when I said I can't dive for shit," he said.

She shrugged. "So use the steps or jump in."

"I'm not that hopeless."

"Come on, stop stalling and get undressed."

She moved to the diving block at the head of the fast lane while he undressed. He watched her tug her goggles into place and step onto the block. Despite the cold wind and the gooseflesh prickling his arms, he felt a thrill as he watched her bend into position. She looked magnificent, all muscle and long legs and coiled potential. For long seconds she hovered on the verge of exploding off the block, waiting for the lane to be clear. Then she dived, her body arching out over the water for what seemed an impossibly long time before she sliced cleanly into the blue of the pool. He watched her power her way up the lane, marveling at the precision and economy of her stroke.

A particularly chill gust of wind reminded him that he was freezing his proverbials off, and he crossed to the medium lane and dived into the water in his own messy, unaccomplished way.

He'd had enough after ten laps. Running kept him fit, but swimming made different demands on his body. He hauled himself out of the pool and dried off, searching for Poppy's blond head in the water. He found her at the far end of the pool, surrounded by half a dozen young swimmers. A middle-aged woman who he guessed was their coach squatted on the deck, her face intent as she listened to Poppy talk to the swimmers. Jake watched as Poppy lifted her arms, demonstrating a stroke technique. The children all imitated her, their small faces filled with reverent awe as they looked at her. Poppy reached out to correct the angle of one boy's arm, talking all the while. The boy laughed, but Jake saw he kept his elbow high as Poppy had shown him when he tried the stroke again.

Poppy looked up and caught Jake's eye. She signaled that she would be with him shortly, and he signaled back that she should take her time. He was almost fully dressed by the time she joined him on the wooden bleachers beside the pool.

"Sorry. I got caught up. Sally—that's the coach for the under-fourteens—keeps asking my advice when she sees me down here. It's becoming a bit of a habit."

"They like you."

She shrugged as she pulled on her sweatpants. "I've been on TV."

"You're a hero, Poppy. They probably have posters of you on their walls at home."

She looked startled at the thought, then she smiled the sweetest, shyest smile he'd ever seen. "Maybe. They're good kids. Some of them can really swim."

She led him to the café and they ate pancakes with berries, surrounded by the high-pitched squeals of children from the indoor pool and the warm, humid smell of chlorine.

They talked about work on the way back to her apartment block, their steps slowing as they approached his car.

"Well. Thanks for giving me the opportunity to freeze my ass off," he said.

"It wasn't that bad."

"You're only saying that because you didn't see my dive."

"I did, actually."

"And?"

She held her hand out palm down and seesawed it back and forth. "So-so. I've seen worse."

"Let me guess. In the five-year-old class?"

Her smile turned into a grin. "Seven-year-old, actually."

"Hmm."

They smiled at each other. Sunlight filtered through the bare branches overhead, brushing her cheek, setting her hair on fire. He didn't want to go home.

He pulled his car keys from his pocket. "Well. I guess I'd better get going."

He waited for her to say something, give him an excuse to come back upstairs with her.

"Yeah. Thanks for the lift home last night," she said. "And for the help with the Hannam article."

"Always so well mannered, Birmingham," he said, shaking his head.

"Always so rude, Stevens."

Even though he wasn't certain she'd welcome it, he ducked his head and kissed her. No tongue, just warm lips and a too-brief taste of her.

"I'll see you later, Poppy."

"Sure."

He got in his car, dumping his wet gear on the passenger side floor mat. Poppy waved once before turning to walk up the path to her apartment.

He pulled away from the curb, hands tight on the wheel.

This is already getting out of hand.

The thing was, after a night in her arms, he couldn't remember exactly why that was such a bad idea anymore.

9

POPPY SPENT SATURDAY tidying her apartment and catching up on her homework for school. Every time her phone rang her heart leaped, even though she told herself that there was no way she would hear from Jake again that weekend.

She was wrong. He called at six that night and they went out for dinner before going to his place. Sunday night they went to an Al Pacino double feature at an old Art Deco cinema near Jake's house and wound up necking in the back row and making love in Jake's car because they couldn't wait to make it home. She left his bed at two in the morning to get some sleep before starting the working week.

She had no idea what was going on between the two of them—great sex, definitely. But there was more to it than that, too.

She felt incredibly self-conscious when she entered the newsroom the next morning, late for the first time since she'd started at the *Herald*. She hadn't given much thought to work during the weekend, how things might play out, how she might feel. Perhaps she should have. She felt as though there was a flashing neon sign above her head announcing that she and Jake had spent the past two days skin to skin.

She kept her head down, but she couldn't resist shooting a quick glance toward Jake as she sat at her desk. He had his back to her as he wrote something in a notepad, one elbow braced on his desk. She studied the breadth of his shoulders, the subtle strength of his arms. His dark hair just brushed the collar of his shirt, the ends curling slightly. She knew exactly how soft that hair was, what it felt like in her hands, against her skin…

She was staring. She forced her gaze away and concentrated on unpacking her bag. The last thing she wanted or needed was people at work guessing what had happened between them. If this was a mistake—and despite how he made her feel, how drawn she was to him, she suspected it was—then she wanted it to be a private one, not a public debacle open to her colleagues' scrutiny and discussion.

She straightened her in-tray, untangled her phone cord. Dusted her computer monitor, culled the out-of-date sticky notes from her diary. Only then did she allow herself to look at Jake again.

He was still writing in his notebook. She wondered if he'd even noticed her arrival, if he was as acutely conscious of her as she was of him.

Stop staring and do some work. Because that's where you are: at work. Where people do stuff other than stare at their lovers.

This was new territory for her, all of it. The hot need he inspired in her. The nature of their relationship, if it could even be called that. The fact that they worked with each other. Her previous life of discipline and focus had left her woefully unprepared to deal with these kinds of situations. Which was probably why she felt so out of control.

She concentrated on calling up a new file and saving it. She had a profile on an up-and-coming runner to write, and she frowned over the notes she'd taken from the interview. Out of the corner of her eye, she registered movement. Her whole body tensed as Jake pushed back his chair and stood. He turned toward the kitchen, started walking. She held her breath, lifted her gaze as he passed her desk. Waited for him to make eye contact or smile, do something to acknowledge that the weekend had really happened.

He was almost past the point of no return when he turned his head toward her. He nodded once, briefly, his gaze glancing over her face.

"Hey," he said.

Then he was gone.

She stared after him.

Hey. That was it? That was all she got after half a dozen orgasms, two movies, dinner and some seriously funny pillow talk?

She turned to her article but all she did was frown at the screen.

What were you expecting? A declaration of love?

No. But she hadn't expected *Hey,* either.

It was a long day. She had to stop herself from staring at Jake in their department meeting. At lunchtime, she went down to the café and ate her lunch two tables away from him, pretending she didn't care that he was sitting and talking and laughing with Jonesy and Davo.

By the time Jake threw her a casual goodbye wave just after six and headed for the elevator, she understood why workplace romances were frowned upon. She'd been unfocused and distracted all day, had a headache that wouldn't quit and was so confused she didn't know where to put herself.

Then she stepped out of the elevator into the underground garage and saw the note folded under her windshield wiper and her stomach lurched with excitement.

Pathetic, Birmingham. Really, really sad.

She waited until she was in the relative privacy of her car before unfolding the note. She stared at the single line:

Dinner after your swim? J.

A more sophisticated woman would wait awhile before texting to accept such a last-minute invitation. Poppy dug her phone out of her bag and sent a quick confirmation.

It wasn't simply that he wanted to see her, despite his cool demeanor all day. He'd remembered that she swam every day. A small thing, perhaps, but it felt as though it meant something. At the very least, it meant he listened to what she said, remembered it.

Yes. That had to mean something.

THEY SAW EACH OTHER every night that week, even Tuesday night when Poppy had night school till nine. By Friday, she was growing used to Jake's cool friendliness at work. It still gave her pause when he treated her as casually as he did everyone else, but she knew it was smart to keep their private life private. After all, the odds were good this thing of theirs had only a finite lifespan. This way, she got to keep her dignity afterward.

Friday night, Jake took her to an out-of-the-way Malaysian restaurant he'd been hearing good things about. They both went into raptures over the pork in coffee sauce and tamarind prawns and Jake insisted she try a Malaysian beer with their meal.

"It's what the locals drink. It makes the experience authentic," he said.

She obliged him by taking a mouthful from his glass.

"Okay, it's nice," she conceded. "Even though I am no a beer fan."

"And you call yourself an Australian."

"I know. It's my dirty little secret."

"What other dark truths lurk in your soul, Poppy Birmingham?" Jake asked, leaning toward her. "Hmm?"

His eyes were bright with laughter, his hair ruffled. He was smiling, one eyebrow quirked in expectation. She stared at him and knew that she'd never meet a more attractive man in her life.

"I don't think I have any dark truths."

"I refuse to accept that. There must be something."

"Sorry, my conscience is clean."

He grinned. "Well, maybe I should make it my mission to dirty it up a little."

"Yeah? How exactly do you plan on doing that?"

"Well, for starters—"

"Poppy! God, of all the places!"

Poppy's head came up at the sound of her sister's voice. Sure enough, Gillian stood beside the neighboring table, about to sit down with a large group of friends.

"Gill," Poppy said. For absolutely no reason, she felt acutely self-conscious. She never, ever ran into her sister or brother around town, mostly because they moved in very different circles. To run into Gillian while she was out with Jake felt…awkward. She wasn't quite sure why.

Gillian's gaze shifted to Jake, then back to Poppy again.

"I've been meaning to call you. How are you doing?" Gill asked. Her sister wiggled her eyebrows meaningfully. She wanted an introduction.

"I'm good. Work's been busy. Um, Gill, this is Jake. Jake, this is my sister, Gill," she said.

Gill turned the full force of her charm on Jake, smiling and offering her hand. "Jake, pleased to meet you. I'm going to be gauche and come right out and say I'm a big fan of your book. I work in publishing and I still think it's one of the best Australian novels of the last decade."

Jake sat back a little in his chair. "Nice of you to say so."

Even though his face was completely impassive, Poppy could feel his discomfort. He didn't like talking about his writing. She'd never really registered it before, but it was true.

"Well, I'm not the only one to say so. I was talking to Robert Hughes the other day and he was raving about you, wondering why we haven't seen a second novel yet," Gill said, shamelessly dropping the name of Australia's foremost art critic.

"You know how it is, life gets in the way," Jake said.

Gillian propped her hand on her hip and gave him an appraising look, a half smile on her lips. Poppy could see her sister was about to launch into a full interrogation, despite Jake's patent reluctance. She did the only thing she could think of—she reached across the table, took Jake's hand in hers and smiled at her sister.

"Have you been here before? The food is really great. Jake's friend recommended it to him, otherwise we never would have heard about it. Which I'm glad we did, because, honestly, the coffee pork is to die for." She was talking too fast, had said too much, but her sister took the hint.

Gill's gaze rested on their joined hands for a moment before lifting to Poppy's face.

"No, I haven't. But I've heard a lot of good things." She turned to Jake. "It was nice to meet you. We should do lunch or something soon, Poppy."

"Sure," Poppy said easily.

Gill rejoined her friends, and Poppy tried to ease her hand from Jake's. His fingers curled around hers, refusing to let go. She met his eyes and saw he was smiling at her.

"Slaying my dragons for me, Poppy?"

She shrugged, embarrassed. "She can be a bit scary some-times. And I could tell you didn't want to talk about it."

He turned her hand over and lifted it to press a kiss into her palm. Her breath caught in her throat as he looked at her.

"Thank you."

Warmth expanded in her chest. When he looked at her like that…

Finally he let her hand go. She tucked it into her lap, still feeling the brush of his lips against her skin.

"So, where does the Amazonian gene come from? Is your brother blond like you?" he asked.

"Nope. He's small and dark, like the rest of them. Charlie said I was a throwback to our long-lost Viking heritage."

Jake smiled. "Poppy the Conqueror. Yeah, I can see you wearing a helmet with horns, waving a big sword around."

"Thank you. I think that's the nicest thing anyone's said to me all day," she said drily.

He laughed. She loved that he got her jokes. And she loved the way his gaze kept dropping to the neckline of her shirt, making her think of what would happen when they got home. She especially loved the way he'd looked at her just now, his gaze warm and intense.

"I'm going to go powder my nose," she said.

She wove her way through the crowded dining room to the restrooms. When she exited the cubicle to wash her hands, her sister was standing by the hand basin.

"Gill," Poppy said, not really surprised to see her. They weren't the closest of sisters, but she knew Gill was interested in Jake because of who he was.

"Poppy, you dark horse. I thought you and Jake were just friends."

"We were."

"But you're not anymore?"

"Um, no. I guess not." Poppy shuffled from one foot to the other. She'd never been the kind of woman who talked about her sex life with friends.

Gill eyed her speculatively as Poppy washed her hands. "He's much better looking in real life."

"Yes."

"Very sexy."

"Mmm."

"Well, Mom will be thrilled. She'll get to grill him properly now."

"Oh, no. It's not like that. We're just… It's very casual. Very," Poppy explained. The last thing she wanted was her mother on the phone, asking twenty questions about her literary boyfriend.

Gill frowned. "That doesn't sound like you."

"First time for everything." Poppy made a point of checking her watch. "Better get back to the table…"

Gill caught her arm before she could go. "Poppy, wait a minute." Gill searched Poppy's face, her eyes concerned. "Are you sure you know what you're doing?"

"Of course. I *have* had sex before, you know."

"In a relationship, though, right?"

"Honestly, Gill…"

"I'm only asking because I don't want you to get hurt."

"I won't. I know exactly what this is. Jake's not up for anything serious. He made that clear up front."

"And what about you? What are you up for?"

Poppy shrugged. "I'm going along for the ride."

Gill studied her face for a long moment. "Well, I hope that's true. Because if you're hanging in there, hoping your casual thing will turn into something less casual, you're setting yourself up to be hurt, Poppy. Believe me, I've been there, and if there's one piece of advice I can give you, it's to believe a man when he says he's not interested in having a relationship. Women always think they know better, or that once the guy gets to know them that rule won't apply to them, but it always does."

For a moment Poppy could see every one of her sister's thirty-five years in the lines around Gill's eyes and mouth. Then Gill patted her arm.

"Sorry—here endeth the lesson, I promise. Have fun with your sexy writer. And look after yourself, Poppy."

She kissed Poppy's cheek and gave her a brief hug, both enormously demonstrative gestures for her typically stand-offish sister.

"I will. You, too," Poppy said.

Jake was talking on his cell phone as she picked her way through the dining room to their table. She watched as he laughed at something his caller said, then started talking animatedly.

He was so damned *compelling*, it almost hurt her to look at him.

Her sister's words echoed in her mind: *you're setting yourself up to be hurt, Poppy.*

She lifted her chin. She wasn't stupid. She knew the score. As long as she kept reminding herself that what was happening between her and Jake was about sex and nothing else, she would be fine.

Absolutely. And in the meantime, she would have fun. After years of swimming drills and discipline, she figured she'd earned a little.

THE FOLLOWING SATURDAY, Jake poured himself a cup of strong black coffee and walked to the living room to sit at his desk. He'd just returned from Poppy's. She'd been headed for the pool as he left, a towel slung over her shoulder, long legs eating up the sidewalk.

He'd been tempted to join her, but he had to polish a feature on Australian cricketing greats that was due on Monday. For the first time in a long time, he resented the fact that his work often bled into his personal life. Maybe because for the first time in a long time he actually had a personal life. Today, for example, it would have been nice to swim with Poppy, then take her to the old Abbotsford Convent, where he'd heard there was an organic bakery and a vegetarian restaurant. Poppy would get off on the healthy food, and afterward they could walk around and look at the old buildings. Instead, he was writing about Donald Bradman and Dennis Lillee.

Jake frowned and took a mouthful of coffee. He was thinking about Poppy way too much. Making plans in his head, coming up with new places to take her, things she might enjoy. For a casual thing, their relationship had quickly taken on a life of its own.

He had no idea what he was doing. Every day he told himself to back off, take it easy with her. And every day he found an excuse to touch her, to be with her. He wasn't ready to give her up yet. He knew he would have to, eventually, but right now he didn't have it in him to walk away.

He forced himself to focus and two hours later he hit Save for the last time. According to his complaining belly, it was well past lunchtime. He stood and stretched, then walked into the kitchen in search of food. He hadn't been shopping all week, so it was probably going to have to be cereal or toast. He opened the freezer to make sure he had no frozen pizzas left and barked out a laugh when he saw what was in there—

a neat stack of frozen meals, a sticky note stuck to one of the boxes. He smiled as he read Poppy's sloping, messy scrawl:

In case of nutritional emergency, break box and heat contents. Then get your pitiful bachelor ass to the supermarket to buy some real food.

He wondered when she'd sneaked the meals into his freezer, then remembered he'd jumped into the shower to wash off the sweat from his run shortly after she arrived on Wednesday night.

"Sneaky," he said into the depths of his freezer.

He chose a stir-fry dish, pierced the top and popped it into the microwave. Then he reached for the phone and dialed her number.

She answered on the third ring.

"Hey," she said.

"Hey, yourself. Ask me what I'm having for lunch."

He leaned a hip against the door frame and slid his free hand into the front pocket of his jeans.

"Lunch? Oh, right. You found the meals."

"Pretty sneaky, getting them into my freezer without me noticing. Ever thought about a career in industrial espionage?"

"Every other day."

"Worried about me starving to death, Poppy?"

"Just making sure you keep your strength up. For entirely selfish purposes. Don't want you passing out at a vital moment or anything."

"Hmm. I guess I should probably return the favor. Keep your strength up, blah blah."

"Well, you know my great love of frozen food," she said with heavy irony.

He grinned. He could imagine the exact look she had in her eyes, the tilt to her head.

"You've been ruined by years of good nutrition, that's your problem."

"Yeah, it's a killer."

"Come to dinner," he said. "I'll cook you something nice."

There was a short pause. He frowned.

"If you have other plans, we can do it another night," he said, even though what he really wanted to ask was what she was doing and who she was doing it with.

"What time do you want me?"

His shoulders relaxed. "Seven. How does that sound?"

"Okay. I'd better get out of this wet swimsuit. Wash the chlorine off."

"Sure. I'll see you later."

He ended the call and stared at the receiver for a few minutes. He hadn't planned on seeing her tonight, but now he was. He shrugged. Poppy was a big girl, she could take care of herself. If she didn't want to see him, she'd say so.

HE SPENT THE REST OF THE afternoon doing some much-needed laundry. At four he went out for groceries. It was close to seven and the kitchen was rich with the smell of baking lasagna when the phone rang. He wiped his hands on a tea towel before taking the call.

"Jake Stevens."

"Jake."

One word was all it took for him to recognize his ex-wife's voice, even though it had been four years since they last spoke. Slowly, he put down the tea towel.

"Marly."

"How are you?"

"I'm good."

"I've been reading your columns. I liked that piece you did on retiring footballers."

"Thanks." He took a deep breath. "Listen, Marly, did you want something?"

There was a small silence on the other end of the line.

"Wow. That's certainly straight to the point."

"Sorry." He pinched the bridge of his nose. It had been five years since the divorce, and he still couldn't talk to her without feeling the old tension in his chest.

"It's all right. We haven't exactly been on talking terms, have we?"

"No."

"That's kind of why I'm calling, actually. I know you still see Marian and Paul sometimes, and I didn't want you hearing it from them." She paused. "I'm pregnant."

He should have expected it. What other reason would she have for calling, after all? She and Gavin had been married for two years now, they'd probably been trying for a while. It was only natural that having a baby together would be high on their list of priorities.

But still he felt winded.

"Jake? Hello?"

He took a deep breath and pulled himself together.

"Congratulations. When are you due?"

That was what he was supposed to ask, right? There was no way he could ask the other questions crowding his mind. Are you still going to call the baby Emma if it's a girl and Harry if it's a boy? Do you still want a natural birth?

Will it make you forget the baby we lost?

"I'm twenty weeks. Halfway."

Four weeks past the point when she'd miscarried last time.

"That's great. Everything good? Mother and baby both well?" he asked.

"Yes."

"Well. I'm happy for you."

"Gavin's taken some time off work and we're going to take it easy for the last few months. Just to make sure everything is okay this time," Marly said.

He closed his eyes, hearing the implied criticism in her tone. Even now, she couldn't let it go.

"Should give you plenty of time to prepare for the baby," he said neutrally.

She was silent for a beat. He could hear her breathing on the other end of the line.

"Do you ever think about her?" she finally asked.

"Yes. Of course I do."

"She'd be six years old. In grade one at school." She was crying, her voice breaking.

"Marly…"

"I'm sorry. It's just been on my mind a lot lately. For obvious reasons."

"Sure."

"Anyway, I'll let you go. Stay well, Jake."

"I'll keep an eye out in the paper for the announcement," he said.

He ended the call. For a long moment he simply stood there, trying to keep a lid on all the shit she'd stirred up.

It was amazing, but even after five years he still felt the tug of responsibility toward her. The tears in her voice, the thread of misery—like Pavlov's dogs, all the old instincts roared to life inside him. The need to make her happy, to heal her, to somehow find the one magic thing that would make it all okay.

The old anger was there, too. Anger at himself, for not being around when she needed him. Anger at her for not being stronger. Anger at life for throwing more misery at them than they'd been able to handle.

Memories he'd thought long buried rose: the emptiness in Marly's eyes when he'd finally arrived at the hospital after she'd lost their baby; the oppressive darkness of their bedroom for months afterward, Marly curled on the bed day after day. And finally Marly's body stretched on the bathroom floor, pale and lifeless.

He swore under his breath and strode to the living room. He didn't know where to put himself. He didn't want to relive this shit. He wanted it gone, forgotten. But all the old stuff was welling up inside him.

Why the hell had she called? He didn't need to know she was having another baby. It was none of his business. Nothing to do with him.

His movements jerky, he grabbed a bottle of wine and pulled the cork. He was taking his first mouthful when the doorbell rang.

It took him a moment to remember that he'd invited Poppy over.

Shit.

He passed a hand over his face and took a deep breath. Then he went to open the door.

"Hey," she said brightly. She held up a supermarket bag. "I brought ice cream for dessert."

He forced a smile.

"Great. Come on in. The lasagna's almost done."

She followed him into the kitchen and unloaded a tub of chocolate-chip ice cream onto the counter. He shoved it into the freezer and grabbed another wineglass. All the while he avoided her eyes. If he looked at her, he was afraid it would all come tumbling out—all the misery, all the grief, all the anger.

"Did you get your article finished?" she asked as he poured her a drink.

"Yes."

He slid her glass across the counter. The wine slopped dangerously close to the rim.

"Is there anything I can do to help?" She looked expectantly around the kitchen.

"You know what, why don't you go to the living room and find something to put on the stereo while I make the salad?"

He felt as though his skin was too tight, as though one wrong word or gesture would shred what little control he had.

She hesitated for a moment.

"Sure, no worries. I'll leave you to it."

Once she was gone, he braced his arms against the counter and hung his head.

It's the past. It's gone. It doesn't mean anything.

"Jake, is everything okay?" Poppy asked quietly from behind him.

He straightened. She was standing in the doorway, a wrinkle of concern on her forehead.

"Did you find something you want to listen to?"

He reached for his wine and took a good swallow. Poppy watched him, her eyes wary.

"If you need to talk… I mean, it's not as though I don't owe you on that front, after Uncle Charlie and everything."

"I'm fine," he said. It came out a little more curtly than he'd meant it to and she flinched.

"Okay." She gave him a small, uncertain smile and returned to the living room.

The timer sounded and he grabbed the oven mitts. He'd

barely got a grip on the stoneware lasagna dish when his wrist contacted one of the hot wire shelves. He jerked away from the pain, and the dish slid from his hands and hit the tiled floor with a crack. Lasagna went everywhere.

"Shit. Bloody hell."

He threw the oven mitts to one side and sucked on the burn on his wrist. Couldn't he catch one freaking break tonight? Was that too much to ask?

"You've hurt yourself. Let me see."

Poppy was in the room, reaching for his arm. He pulled away, unable to tolerate her gentle sympathy.

For a moment they were both very quiet. Then she took a step backward.

"Listen, Jake. If this is a bad time for you, I can always go home."

He stared at the mess on the floor. His chest ached with guilt and anger and grief.

"Yeah. Maybe that's a good idea."

She blinked and he realized she hadn't expected him to take her up on her offer.

"Okay. I guess I'll see you at work, then."

He moved to walk her to the door. She held up a hand.

"It's fine. I know the way out," she said.

She was gone then, the front door closing behind her with a decisive click.

He swore again and closed his eyes.

He'd hurt her feelings. Again.

Grim, he squatted and used the tea towel to scoop the bulk of the ruined lasagna into the two halves of the dish. He dumped the lot in the sink then decided the rest could wait till morning. He needed to get out of the house.

He grabbed his car keys and his wallet and took the

stairs to the back of the building where his Porsche was parked.

He shot out into the street and wove through the traffic, working his way north and east until he was turning into the darkened road leading into Studley Park. Just four kilometers from the city center, the park sprawled over more than six hundred acres and featured one of Melbourne's most challenging roads. Jake put his foot down and took the first corner hard. The Porsche growled beneath him as he changed down a gear and punched the accelerator.

By the time he roared to a stop at the lookout point, he'd wrestled his way around enough corners to take the edge off. The engine quieted to a low rumble, then fell silent as he switched it off.

He walked to the lone picnic bench at the lookout, cold wind biting through his sweater. He sat on the table, feet on the bench seat, elbows braced on his knees. He stared out at the city spread below—the towering skyscrapers, the many twinkling lights of the sprawling suburbs, the constantly moving red-and-white dots of cars on the roads.

Marly had caught him off guard with her news, but it scared him how quickly the old shit had come up at him. He'd thought he'd put it all behind him. Wanted to, more than anything. He'd taken what lessons he could from the experience and moved on.

So why was he sitting up here alone, tears burning at the back of his eyes as he thought about the child he'd lost and his broken marriage?

He stood and walked to the very edge of the lookout, right to the safety barrier where the land fell away abruptly.

Shit happens, man. Deal with it.

It had been his motto for the long months of Marly's depression. Deal with her silence. Deal with her tears. Deal with her accusations and blame. Deal with her attempt to take her own life.

The truth was, he'd spent so much time looking after her, he'd barely had time to feel anything for himself. But someone had had to be the strong one.

Slowly the churning in his gut settled. He returned to the picnic table and sat, breathing in the cool night air. Inevitably, his thoughts turned to Poppy.

He'd hurt her, the way he'd pushed her away. He scrubbed his face with his hands. Maybe it was for the best. The past few weeks had been crazy, but maybe now was the time to start being smart. Before great sex turned into something more than it was ever meant to be.

He stared at the night sky and thought about cutting Poppy out of his life. About never touching her again. Never laughing with her, never teasing her.

Letting her go, before she got hurt.

He turned and went back to his car.

HE'D LET HER WALK OUT the door so easily. That was what killed her the most.

Poppy pushed away the untouched bowl of pasta she'd made for herself and stared at the worn spot on the arm of her couch.

He'd been upset, wounded in some way. She'd seen it in his eyes, his face, the moment he'd opened the door to her. And instead of seeking comfort from her, instead of sharing or taking solace, he'd blocked her out. Literally kicked her out of his kitchen, then let her walk away when she offered to give him space.

Shouldn't have offered to leave if you didn't mean it, her cynical self said.

She'd wanted him to talk to her—that was why she'd offered to leave. She hadn't expected him to let her go.

Which said a lot about the dynamics of their relationship.

Time to face the music, Poppy.

She took a deep breath and then let it out again.

She wanted more from Jake than he was willing to give. This wasn't casual for her. Maybe it never had been.

And she knew, absolutely, that Jake did not feel the same way. Even though things had been pretty damn intense between them the past few weeks, even though when they were together they laughed and had great sex and interesting discussions about everything under the sun, there was always a part of Jake that was constantly checking the exits, in case he had to leave in a hurry. He was drawn to her despite himself, a reluctant recruit to their mutual attraction.

What was it her sister had said?

If there's one piece of advice I can give you, it's to believe a man when he says he's not interested in having a relationship.

Good advice. Pity Poppy had already been too far gone by then to take it.

Poppy pulled her legs tight to her chest and rested her chin on her knees. This was new territory for her, this aching vulnerability, this tenderness. It scared her, because she knew there was a part of her that wanted Jake so much that she'd take whatever scraps of himself he was willing to throw her way. And she might not be an expert on relationships or love, but she knew that that way lay great heartache.

The doorbell rang. She stared down the hallway. It was Jake. It had to be—it was nearly ten and she couldn't think of anyone else who'd come calling unannounced at this time of night.

Plus, her heart was racing. Usually a reliable sign he was somewhere in the vicinity.

All the same, she checked the peephole before opening the door, just in case. Jake stood in profile to her, his head down. He was holding flowers. His expression was unreadable, utterly neutral.

She rested her forehead against the cool surface of the door for a second, love for him washing over her. She wanted to open the door and cling to him, press her face into his neck and inhale his smell, wrap her body around his, get as close as it was humanly possible for two people to be.

She was such an idiot.

It had crept up on her when she wasn't looking, but it had probably been inevitable from the moment she asked him to stay the night. She wasn't the kind of woman who could be casual with her body or her feelings. Her sister had seen it—and deep in her heart, Poppy had known, too.

She took a deep breath. Then she opened the door. Jake swung to face her. Up close his eyes were watchful, wary. He offered her the flowers.

"I'm a dick. I was having a bad day. I shouldn't have taken it out on you," he said simply.

She stared at the flowers, then his face, wanting more. Some small sign that he trusted her. That this was about more than sex for him. That the ache in her chest was not about to become a permanent fixture.

His mouth quirked into a half smile. "If you're interested, there's a little café in Fitzroy that serves great lasagna. Even better than the stuff I scraped off my kitchen floor."

She waited, but there was nothing more.

So.

He wasn't going to give her a reason why.

He wasn't going to share his pain with her, the way she'd shared hers with him.

It's early days yet. He's wary. He's obviously had a bad divorce. Give him time.

Of course, it was also entirely possible that the only part of himself that Jake would ever willingly share with her was his penis, and that holding out for more would only make the inevitable that much more painful.

"Can I come in?" Jake asked.

She realized she'd been standing staring at him for a long time. Slowly, she stepped to one side.

She followed him to the living room and watched him take in the abandoned bowl of spaghetti on her coffee table.

"You've eaten already," he said.

"Yes."

End it. End it now. Save yourself a world of disappointment. End it while you can still look him in the eye and be his friend and work with him.

Her sensible self, speaking with her sister's voice.

She stared at the flowers in her hand. They were something, right? He'd gone to the trouble of finding a florist that was open at this time of night. He could have shown up empty-handed, or gotten some nasty, limp bouquet from the gas station.

She looked at him.

"There's some spaghetti left, if you want it. I could heat it in the microwave."

"Yeah? To be honest, I'm starving," he said. He looked tired. She wanted to cup his face in her hands and draw the pain out of him.

Instead, she went into the kitchen and took the bowl of leftover pasta from the fridge. She could feel him watching her as she put cling film over the bowl and set the microwave timer, but she deliberately didn't look at him. She needed a few seconds to get her game face on. The last thing she wanted was for him to look into her eyes and understand she'd fallen in love with him.

He was studying the dancing monkeys on her baggy old pajamas when she turned around.

"I'm not exactly dressed for company," she said.

His eyes were warm on her from across the small room. "Come here."

When she didn't move, he reached out and caught her elbow, tugging her toward him.

"The spaghetti…"

"I came here for you, not for food."

He kissed her then, his hands cradling her head, and she closed her eyes against the tide of longing and need that rose inside her. One kiss, one caress was all it ever took with Jake.

"I'm sorry, okay?" he said against her mouth. "I was an asshole. It won't happen again, I promise."

He held her eyes until she nodded.

"I'll hold you to it," she said.

"Good."

They kissed again and he slid his hands down her back and beneath the waistband of her pajamas. She shivered as his hands cupped her bare backside, his fingers curving beneath her cheeks.

"No underwear, Ms. Birmingham?"

"As I said, I wasn't expecting company."

"So this is what you get up to when you're on your own, swan around the apartment commando?"

"George likes it that way."

He grinned and backed her against the kitchen counter. "George. I was kind of hoping he was off the scene."

He was, but she wasn't about to tell Jake that he'd ruined her for all other forms of pleasure.

He slid his knee between her legs, nudging them apart. One of his hands found the buttons on her pajama top and he slid them free while he kissed the tender skin beneath her ear, his tongue sending prickles of desire racing through her body.

He murmured his appreciation as he bared her breasts, then he lowered his head and she let her head drop back as he pulled a nipple into his mouth.

He felt so good. She was so ready for him it hurt.

She fumbled with his belt, then his fly. He took care of protection while she kicked her pajama pants off, then she lifted her leg over his hip and he pushed inside her, big and thick and long.

She clutched his bare ass, holding him still inside her for a few precious seconds, savoring the moment. Then he started to move, his cock stroking her, the friction exquisite. His backside flexed and contracted beneath her hands. His breathing became ragged. She could hear the sounds of their bodies meeting and parting, could feel the hot wetness of her own desire.

She pressed her face close to his chest and inhaled, consciously absorbing his smell, the feel of his skin against hers, the power of his body as he pressed himself into her.

I love you, she told him in her mind as she pulled his hips closer, urging him inside her. *I love you, Jake Stevens.*

He kissed her, his tongue sweeping her mouth, his lips teasing hers. She held her breath. Tensed. Closed her eyes.

Then her body was pulsing with pleasure, wave after wave washing over her. She clutched him to her, calling his name over and over. She felt him tense. His body stroked into hers one last time. He shuddered, his body as hard as granite as he came.

For a moment there was only the sound of their harsh breathing. Then Jake drew back a little so he could look down into her face.

"I think the spaghetti is done," he said.

She hadn't even heard the timer sound. Amusement danced in his eyes, along with something else. Something warm and real. Something that made her fiercely glad that she'd let him in, despite the lack of explanation and her realization that she was far more invested in their relationship than he was.

He cares. He may not love me yet, but he cares.

He smoothed her hair from her forehead with his thumb. Then he kissed the corner of her mouth and withdrew from her. She listened to the heavy tread of his footsteps as he headed for the bathroom.

She closed her eyes for a moment, savoring the satisfied pulse of her body. Maybe she was stupid. Maybe she was going to get hurt, but so be it. Right now, right this minute, she'd take what she could get of Jake Stevens and hope like hell that the warmth she saw sometimes when he looked at her was not wishful thinking and self-delusion.

And maybe next time he was troubled or his demons came calling, he would turn *to* her instead of away.

10

THE NEXT MORNING, JAKE woke with words in his head. Poppy was breathing deeply beside him, still asleep, and he kept his eyes closed as images and ideas swirled in his mind. Slowly, the words became phrases, then sentences. He shuffled them in his head like a deck of cards. More words came to him. His fingers itched to pick up a pen and find some paper.

It had been so long since he'd woken like this, he was almost afraid. Once, it had been commonplace, a part of his world. But he hadn't wanted to write, needed to write, for a long time.

Finally the urge to put it down on paper became too much for him. He eased out of bed, tugged on his boxer briefs and went to the living room. Poppy kept scrap paper by the phone to take down messages and he helped himself to a few pages. He sat at her dining room table and started to write. After a few minutes, he stood and grabbed more paper. A few sheets wasn't going to be enough. He felt as though a floodgate had opened inside him. The words and images were flowing fast and he needed to get them down.

His hand flew across the page. Twenty minutes in, his fingers began to cramp. He shook them out and kept writing.

"Hey. You're up early."

Poppy stood in the doorway, a T-shirt barely skimming the

tops of her thighs. Her hair was ruffled and there was a crease on her face from the pillow.

"Couldn't sleep," he said.

Her gaze dropped to the pages of closely written script in front of him. There was a question in her eyes when she raised them to his face. He shrugged self-consciously.

"An idea for work," he said.

"Ah. I was wondering what had you so fired up so early."

He felt bad for lying to her, but the truth was that he didn't know what this was yet. He started gathering the pages together.

"You want cereal or toast?" she asked as she moved toward the kitchen.

He shook his head, standing. "I'm all right, thanks." He went to the bedroom and began pulling on his clothes.

Poppy looked surprised when he stepped into the living room, fully dressed, pages folded into his back pocket.

"You're going?"

"I've got some things I need to do," he said. "But I'll call you this afternoon, okay?"

She nodded. "Sure."

He kissed her goodbye, savoring the cool softness of her cheek against his. Then he was heading down the stairs, his mind full of more words, more ideas.

He spent the day writing. A story was starting to emerge from the conversations and scenes he'd woken with. The man in his story took on flesh, found his voice. The woman, too.

It wasn't until she became pregnant that Jake understood what he was doing. His fingers slowed on the keyboard then stopped. He stared at the screen.

He couldn't write this. Could he?

But already he knew where he wanted to go next, what he needed to put on the page. He wanted to tell it all, every ugly, sad, messy moment of it. He wanted to lay it all out on clean white paper and sweep it out of the dark corners of his mind.

No one need ever read it. Certainly he would never publish it—it was too raw, too personal. But maybe it was something he needed to do. And since it was the first time he'd felt the urge to write in years, it didn't feel as though he had a choice. Not if he ever wanted to reclaim his life.

He took a deep breath. Then he started to write.

TWO WEEKS LATER, POPPY LAY on her bed and watched the morning sun paint patterns on the far wall.

Her body was warm and languid from Jake's lovemaking, her blood still thrumming through her veins. She turned her head and stared at the hollow his head had left in the pillow. She could hear him in the bathroom down the hall, singing his version of Madonna's "Like a Virgin" while he showered. She smiled as he reached for a high note.

That was the thing about Jake. He could always make her laugh, be it with an arrogant comment, a smart-ass quip or boyish stupidity. It was one of the things she loved about him.

The list was growing longer by the day.

Don't start, Birmingham.

She pulled the sheet up to cover her breasts and grabbed his pillow, piling it behind herself before reaching for the book she was reading. It was a Saturday and she didn't have to be anywhere in a hurry. In the bathroom, Jake switched to Nina Simone.

Two weeks ago, she would have been in there with him, but staying in bed this morning and letting him shower alone was today's proof to herself that she could live without Jake Stevens in her life. She made a point of doing something every day to reassure herself that she could. She might love him, but she could live without him. And she would. If she had to.

Loving Jake was like riding a roller coaster. Sometimes when he looked at her, she was so sure she saw something more than lust in his eyes. She had no doubt that he liked her, that he enjoyed spending time with her. He cared about her feelings. And he wanted her. If all of that didn't add up to love, it came pretty damn close.

She could almost let herself believe the fantasy. Almost. But she still had no idea what had cut him so deeply the night of their disastrous dinner. And he still hadn't told her what he was working on. A new book, she guessed. But that was only a guess, because he hadn't shared it with her.

She ached to ask him. Just as she ached for him to confide his pain in her. She wanted to share his life, in every sense of the word. But Jake had to want to share it with her, he had to offer himself up—his trust wasn't something she could demand.

The water shut off and she opened her book and started reading. She was doing a credible impression of an engaged reader when Jake came into the room, a towel slung low on his waist. She tried to keep herself from following him with her eyes as he dressed, but she was powerless against her desire for him.

He had a beautiful body, long and strong and lean. Her gaze swept the width of his torso then ran down his spine. He had a great ass, round and firm from running. And his legs were corded with muscle and dusted with crisp, dark hair. He pulled on boxer-briefs and she watched as he adjusted himself.

Man, it got her hot when he touched himself like that.

She shifted in the bed and he glanced at her.

"Good book?" he asked.

She had to flick a look at the cover to remember what she was reading.

"Yeah. It's funny. He's a good writer," she said.

"When are you going to your parents' place?" he asked as he tugged on jeans.

"Early afternoon. Mom and Dad's party isn't till tonight, but I promised I'd help out."

Jake finished buckling his belt and crossed to sit on the side of the bed.

"Drive carefully, okay?" he said.

He took her hand, his thumb running across the top of her knuckles. Her heart swelled in her chest as she looked into his face. He cared. Definitely he cared.

"I've driven that road about a million times," she said.

"Still." He leaned forward and kissed her gently. Then he stood and grabbed his T-shirt from the top of her chest of drawers.

"When do you think you'll be back?"

"I'll probably leave after breakfast tomorrow, be back midmorning. Don't worry, I haven't forgotten your precious Martin Scorsese double feature."

Jake had been eyeing the Sunday matinee all week.

"This is for your edification, not mine. I can't believe you haven't seen *Goodfellas*. It's a classic."

"I'm prepared to be moved."

He grinned. "Oh, you will be."

He finished tying his shoes and straightened. She put down her book.

"Well. I guess I'll see you tomorrow," he said.

"Yep."

This would be the first Saturday night they'd spent apart in four weeks. She wondered if he'd even noticed.

He leaned down to kiss her. She slid her hand around his neck for just a second, holding him close, then she forced herself to let him go.

"See you," she said.

She made herself stay in bed, supremely casual, as he let himself out. Once she'd heard the door close behind him she fell back against the pillows and closed her eyes. She could still smell his deodorant hanging in the air.

"I love you," she told the empty room.

Before she could start thinking things to death, she threw the covers back and hit the shower. If she went to the pool now, she could get her laps done and spend some time helping Sally with the under-fourteens. At least that was one area where she felt on solid ground.

She spent an hour cutting through the water, losing herself in the rhythm of the pool. Sally was teaching her kids tumble turns, and Poppy showed them a few tricks of the trade before showering and hitting the road.

It was nearly midday when she pulled into her parents' driveway. She spent the afternoon helping prepare for their anniversary party. Gill arrived at four with her new boyfriend, Daniel, followed shortly by Adam with his long-term partner, Wendy. Poppy was acutely aware that Uncle Charlie was missing from the family circle as they all stood in the kitchen talking and laughing. For a moment she was overwhelmed with sadness. Then her mother asked for help stirring the gravy and she didn't have time to think until it was time to file into the dining room.

It wasn't until they were all seated that Poppy registered she was the only person without a partner. Normally, Uncle Charlie sat beside her, so she wasn't as aware of her single status. Certainly it had never bothered her before. But tonight she looked around the table and felt her aloneness acutely.

Her sister must have noticed the same thing because she cornered Poppy in the kitchen after dessert.

"I was kind of thinking Jake might be here," she said.

"No."

"Family dinner too dull for him, huh?" Gill asked. She was joking, her attention more than half-focused on cutting herself a second slice of cake.

"I didn't ask him. I figured mentioning a family gathering would be a surefire way to send him running for the hills."

Poppy closed her mouth with a click. Where the hell had that come from?

Gill's face was an advertisement for sisterly concern.

"Oh, Poppy," she said.

Suddenly Poppy was blinking away tears. "I'm fine. It's all good. We're having a good time, no strings."

"Except you want there to be strings."

It wasn't a question. Poppy nodded miserably. It was almost a relief to admit it to someone.

Gill shook her head. "Men are such assholes sometimes."

"I'm the one who broke the rules," Poppy said. "This was supposed to be a casual thing."

"Yeah, right. I told you, didn't I? It always gets messy. If you like a man enough to spend that much time with him, to share your body with him, what the hell is going to stop you from falling all the way in love with him?"

"Excellent question," Poppy said with a watery smile.

Gill grabbed her forearm, very earnest. "Tell him how you feel, Poppy. Don't do what I did. I hung on and hung on with Nathan, hoping and hoping he'd realize he cared. I wasted a year eating my heart out for him, going alone to parties because we weren't a couple despite the fact that we slept with each other all the time, turning away other men because I was always holding out hope that Nathan would get it. And he never did."

Poppy stared at her sister. She remembered Nathan. He was a senior executive at the publishing house where Gill worked

Poppy had been introduced to him once when she'd dropped into the office to pick up her sister for a lunch date.

"I always thought Nathan was only a work colleague," Poppy said.

Gill's smile was tight. "You were right. It just took me a while to work that out."

"I'm sorry things didn't work out for you."

"Hey, it's old news. And Daniel is a sweetie, don't you think?"

"Yeah, he seems great."

Gill squeezed Poppy's arm. "Do yourself a favor—tell Jake how you feel, what you want. At least that way you'll know now, rather than waiting and waiting and finding out down the line that you'll never get what you want."

Poppy shook her head. Even the thought of telling Jake made her belly tense. "It's too soon. It's only been a few weeks."

"It was long enough for *you* to fall in love with *him,* wasn't it?" Gill asked.

Poppy stared at her sister, utterly arrested. She knew Gill was right. In her bones she knew.

Their mother entered, a stack of plates in her hands.

"Your dad's pulling out the liqueur glasses. I think it's going to be one of those nights."

Without giving herself time to stop and think, Poppy turned to her mother.

"Mom, I think I'm going to head back into town," she said.

Her mother frowned. "I thought you were staying the night? And haven't you been drinking?"

"I've had one glass. And there's something I need to do," Poppy said.

Gill met her eyes and gave her an encouraging nod.

Ten minutes later Poppy was on the freeway to Melbourne, her gut churning with nerves. She went over and over what she wanted to say in her head, imagining what Jake might say in response. By the time she hit the city she was half nervous, half terrified.

She had no idea how Jake would react. She was very, very afraid that he would reject her. But there was also a flicker of hope in her heart.

She found a parking spot right in front of his apartment building. She told herself it was a good omen. She figured she needed every scrap of luck she could get right now. Her boots rapped sharply against the marble stairs of his building as she climbed to the second floor. She paused outside his door, her hand fisted, ready to knock.

He wasn't expecting her. She probably should have called, warned him she was on the way.

She knocked. There was a short silence, then she heard the sound of footsteps on the other side of the door.

"Jake," she said.

But it wasn't Jake standing in front of her, it was a tall, elegantly dressed woman in a white silk blouse and tailored black pants. About thirty-five, maybe a little older, her hair long, dark and smooth, her makeup flawless.

Poppy stared. She didn't have it in her to do anything else

Another woman. God, why hadn't she even considered it' It wasn't as though she and Jake had ever discussed being exclusive, after all. She had just assumed...

Which, clearly, had been a stupid, naive thing to do.

"Sorry, Jake's not here right now," the woman said. "Bu he shouldn't be long, if you want to come in and wait?"

Poppy took a step backward.

"No, no. Um, it's okay, I can talk to Jake later. At—a work. I didn't mean to barge in. I should have called."

Dinner burned the back of her throat. While she'd been fal

ing in love with Jake, he'd been…what? Romancing this other woman on the side? Sleeping with her the few nights he hadn't been with Poppy?

"Seriously, he just ducked out. Gerome wouldn't quit whining about there being no beer."

"Hey! I made one comment. Hardly whining," a male voice said, then a dark-haired man in his early forties stepped into view and rested a hand on the woman's shoulder.

Poppy stared at him. Then she stared at his hand. Some of the panicked urgency left her body.

The woman stuck her hand out. "I just realized, I should have introduced myself. You probably think we're breaking into Jake's place or something. I'm Fiona, Jake's sister."

Somehow Poppy managed to clasp Fiona's hand and shake it.

"I'm Poppy. Um, I work with Jake," she said.

"When you're not whipping ass for Australia. I'm Gerome, Fiona's whining, beer-loving husband." He smiled. "I've got to say this, even though you probably hear it all the time, but that was an amazing final in the relay you guys pulled off in Beijing. I nearly wet my pants when you outtouched the Poms to come home with the gold."

Fiona rolled her eyes. "Can't take him anywhere." She waved Poppy forward. "Come in, please. Jake will be angry with us if we let you go before he gets back."

Before Poppy could protest, she was drawn into Jake's apartment. It was only when she followed Fiona into the living room that she saw his sister and husband weren't the only visitors. An older couple sat on the couch, wineglasses on the coffee table in front of them.

"Poppy, these are my parents, Harriet and Bernard Stevens. Guys, this is Poppy Birmingham."

"You don't need to tell us that," Jake's dad said. He stood and offered her his hand. "An honor to meet you. My wife and I are big fans."

Poppy smiled and said something appropriate. At least she hoped it was appropriate—she was too busy trying not to stare at the half-eaten birthday cake on the coffee table. She could just make out the words that had been iced on the cake before someone had cut into it: Happy Birthday, Jake. Her gaze shifted to the crumpled wrapping paper on the floor, then to the stack of obviously new books on one arm of the couch.

It was Jake's birthday. And he hadn't told her. He had his family over from Adelaide, and he hadn't told her.

Why would he? a cynical little voice said in the back of her mind. *You're just the warm body he screws. You're not part of his life. Why would he share his family with you?*

His mom was saying something. Poppy shook her head, tried to focus.

It was too much. She'd come here, ready to bare her soul to him, and he hadn't even bothered to let her know it was his birthday.

"I'm sorry. I—I have to go," she said suddenly, interrupting Jake's mother. The other woman looked startled, but Poppy didn't care. She had to get out of there before she burst into tears in front of a roomful of strangers.

"I'm sure Jake will be here any minute. He said the liquor shop was around the corner. I'll call him," Fiona said, pulling out her cell phone.

"No!" Poppy practically yelled it. They all stared at her. "I'll catch up with Jake another time. There's nothing I need to say that can't wait."

She headed for the door and took the stairs two at a time, desperate to avoid bumping into Jake. If she saw him right now, there was no way she'd be able to stop herself from breaking into big, blubbering, self-pitying tears. She hit the foyer at speed and barreled into the street. Relief hit her as she slid behind the wheel.

She'd made it.

Now she just had to do what needed to be done and learn to live with the consequences of her own foolishness.

THE SIX-PACK OF BEER SWUNG heavily in the bag as Jake climbed the stairs to his apartment. At least now his brother-in-law could stop looking so hangdog about the lack of malt-and-hops-based beverages in the house. He'd have to warn his family that if they planned to ambush him on his birthday again they needed to bring their own drinks or possibly end up disappointed.

He smiled to himself as he pulled his keys from his pocket. He still couldn't believe his sister and his parents had flown all the way from Adelaide to Melbourne to surprise him. Although the "casual" phone call he'd had from his sister during the week was now explained. Crafty bastards.

He let himself into the apartment and shrugged out of his coat.

"Okay, Gerome, you fussy bugger—it's beer o'clock," he said as he walked to the living room.

"See, I told you he'd walk in the door the moment she'd gone," Fiona said. She sounded frustrated. "Your timing has always sucked, Jake."

"Sorry?"

"You just missed your friend," his mother said.

Jake frowned.

"Poppy Birmingham," Gerome explained. "She of the long legs and many gold medals."

"Yeah? Poppy was here? She's supposed to be in Ballarat at her folks' place."

"We told her to wait for you, but she wouldn't stay," his mother said.

"Huh." He pulled his cell phone from his back pocket and dialed her cell. She wouldn't have had time to drive far; she could turn around and come back to meet his family.

He frowned as the call went to voice mail.

"Poppy, it's me," he said. "Give me a call when you get this." He thought for a second. She hadn't said anything, but he'd been very aware that this was her first family occasion without Uncle Charlie being around. Maybe it had been too tough and she'd bailed. "Hope everything went okay tonight."

"She said she'd speak to you tomorrow," Fiona said when he'd ended the call.

"And in the meantime, I believe there are six perfectly good beers calling my name," Gerome said.

Jake handed the bag over, still thinking about Poppy.

"She's very striking," his mother said. "I've only ever seen her on TV but she's got a real presence, hasn't she?"

"Yeah," Jake said. He'd wait until she was home then call her to check everything was okay.

"Why don't I make us some coffee?" his mother said, standing and starting to collect wineglasses.

"I'll get it. What does everyone want?" he asked.

He took orders and his mother followed him into the kitchen, clearly determined to help out. He pulled coffee mugs from the cupboard while she filled the kettle, and all the while his mind was on Poppy. Ten more minutes and he would go into his bedroom and call her, make sure she was all right.

"Jake, I know this makes me the worst sort of interfering mother, but I have to ask. Are you seeing Poppy? Is she your girlfriend?"

He pulled the coffee out of the freezer. "You're right, it does."

His mother gave him a dry look. "Well, tough. I'm your mother and I've been worried about you, so I get a free pass now and then."

"I'm fine," he said.

His mom crossed her arms over her chest and leaned against the sink. "Are you?"

"Yes."

"It seems to me that all you do these days is work. That's all you ever seem to talk about when I call."

"Well, you know, unless I win the lottery that's the way it's probably going to be until I retire."

"Jake, stop bullshitting me. I'm serious here."

He stared at her. His mom never swore.

"Ever since the divorce I feel as though you've forgotten how to really live."

"Mom, I'm fine. I swear. I go out, I do stuff. It's not like I'm some bitter divorcé holed up in my apartment, living off canned food."

His mother walked to the freezer and opened the door like a lawyer inviting the jury to examine exhibit A. Jake stared at the neat stack of frozen meals and pizzas filling the small space.

"Okay, maybe I could eat a little better," he conceded.

His mother looked at him sadly. "I wish I could show you how much you've changed. The look in your eyes, the way you carry yourself—it's as though you're always braced, ready to defend yourself in case someone gets too close."

He didn't know how to respond. What his mother was saying was probably true. His marriage had changed him. Made him wary. Worn him down.

"I'm doing okay, Mom," he said.

"I want you to be doing more than okay. I want you to find someone you can love again, someone who loves you.

I want you to have children and write more beautiful books and live a full life instead of this frozen-dinner existence you've been enduring."

"I'm not getting married again, Mom." He said it very seriously, so she'd know it wasn't open to debate. "I don't want to go through any of that crap ever again."

"But what about love? Companionship? What about having a warm body to wake up next to and someone to share jokes with and someone to rub your feet at night?"

His thoughts flew to Poppy, to the way they'd laughed and kissed and fooled around for an hour in her bed this morning before he'd finally got his ass into the shower.

"Never say never," he heard himself say.

His mother blinked. She didn't look any less surprised than he felt himself. When had his strict no involvement, no commitment policy gotten so ragged around the edges?

"Well. I guess I'm going to have to settle for that, aren't I?" his mother said. She was looking rather pleased with herself. And why not? He'd pretty much confirmed her guess about Poppy.

She left him to finish making the coffee alone. He set out sugar and milk on a tray, his thoughts circling.

So much for keeping Poppy at arm's length. She'd crept into his life a moment at a time, even though he'd been telling himself to back off, to be careful. And now it was too late. He cared. He didn't want their relationship to have an expiry date. He was hooked, well and truly.

He rolled his eyes.

Hell, might as well admit it, while he was being honest with himself: he was probably even in love. Wait until his mother worked that one out. She'd be skipping and singing.

He waited for the old tension to grip him as he faced hi

feelings at last. Loving Marly had been a burden in the end, a weight that he carried with him every minute of every day. He'd been driven by the need to help her, heal her, protect her. And in the end he'd had to let her go. He'd never wanted to go there again.

And yet here he was. Poppy had sneaked under his guard and into his heart while he wasn't looking. He'd thought he was indulging in hot sex and a bit of fun, but all the while he'd been falling for her honesty and earthiness and warmth.

He touched a hand to his chest, but there was no band of tension there, no sense of heaviness in his body. He didn't feel burdened by his feelings for Poppy.

He felt…warm. Grateful. Relieved.

A smile spread across his face.

For the first time in years, he felt hope.

"Damn," he said softly.

He wanted to jump in his car and go find her, but he settled for calling her house. He wasn't about to blurt out his feelings over the phone, but he really needed to hear her voice.

The phone rang and rang before her answering machine picked up. Disappointed, he left another message asking her to call him when she got in.

She didn't. He was half tempted to call her after another hour had passed, but it was late. And there was always tomorrow. His feelings weren't going anywhere, right? They'd still be there when he woke. And so would Poppy, even if he felt a ridiculous, adolescent urge to stand beneath her window and serenade her and make absolutely certain that she was his.

HE TRIED PHONING POPPY again first thing the next morning and got her answering machine once more. He wanted to go straight over to her place, but his parents and Gerome and Fiona had flown all the way from Adelaide to see him. Swallowing his impatience, he took them for breakfast at the café in the nearby Royal Botanic Gardens. His gaze constantly strayed to his cell phone throughout, but still Poppy didn't call. To his great relief, his family decided to check out the galleries and shops after breakfast. Jake walked to his apartment alone, planning to try Poppy one last time before heading over to her place.

He spotted her car in front of his apartment block when he turned the corner. A smile curved his mouth. It had never occurred to him before, but he was always smiling when she was around. She was sunshine in human form—strong and proud and beautiful, and he couldn't believe it had taken him so long to see what was right under his nose.

She got out of her car as he approached. By the time he'd reached her side, she'd removed a bag from the trunk.

"Hey," he said. "I was worried about you."

He leaned in to kiss her, but she turned her cheek so that his lips landed on the side of her jaw. He pulled back to look at her. She met his eyes, her expression utterly impassive.

Something was wrong.

"I came over to return the things you left at my place," she said. "Some underwear and a book or two."

She offered him the bag. He looked at it but didn't take it.

"What's going on?"

"I don't want to do this anymore. Sleep with you, I mean."

He felt as though she'd sucker punched him. For a long moment he just stared at her.

"Where is this coming from?" he finally asked. His voice sounded rough, as though he'd forgotten how to use it all of a sudden. "I thought we were having a good time together."

Her gaze slid over his shoulder. "It was always a casual thing, right? I figure it's run its course."

He shook his head. "No. Something happened." He reached for her arm. "Let's go upstairs, grab some coffee, talk properly."

She shrugged away from him. "There's nothing much to say, is there? We were always only about the sex. Once that got old, this was pretty much inevitable. I'm calling it before it gets messy."

She was so damned matter-of-fact. Utterly unmoved, unemotional.

"I wasn't aware that the sex *had* gotten old," he said. He'd meant to provoke her into something, some sign that she felt something as she stood there, kissing goodbye to the most intense four weeks of his life.

She simply lifted a shoulder. "I wanted to tell you to your face."

She offered the bag again. When he still didn't take it, she placed it by his feet.

"It's been a lot of fun. I hope we can still be friends," she said.

Then she offered him her hand. He stared at it. A handshake. She wanted to shake his hand after all the things they'd done together. After he'd made her sob with pleasure. After he'd kissed and caressed and tasted her all over. After he'd fallen in love with her.

"This is bullshit, Poppy. Tell me what's really going on."

"I'm being smart." She turned toward her car.

"Hang on. You can't just drop your little bombshell and drive off."

She kept walking. "You made the rules, Jake." She sounded resigned and sad.

"Poppy."

"I'll see you tomorrow at work."

She got into her car. He swore and reached for the passenger side door, but it was locked. She pulled out into the street. He started after her, then realized what he was doing. He couldn't chase her car down. And even if he could, it wasn't going to get him anywhere. Poppy had made up her mind. She'd cut him loose.

"Shit."

He stood staring after her, his body tight with frustration. There had been no sign that this was coming, not a hint. Yesterday morning, she'd clawed at his back as he made love to her. She'd laughed with him and promised to call the moment she was back from Ballarat. She'd teased him about the Scorsese double feature.

"Shit."

He walked to the sidewalk and picked up his belongings, staring at his neatly folded boxer-briefs and T-shirts in the bottom of the bag. She'd even cleaned him out of her apartment.

By the time he'd climbed the stairs to his apartment his temper was firing on all cylinders. He kept remembering the distance in her voice, the way she'd offered him her hand as if she was some goddamned business associate or something.

"Bullshit, Poppy. This is bullshit," he said as he threw the shopping bag onto the couch.

She'd said that they'd always been only about the sex, but that wasn't true—that hadn't been true from the first time they slept with each other. They were friends. At the very damned least they were friends, and friends owed each other a little more explanation than a handshake and a casual "so long and thanks for all the orgasms."

He was pretty sure that if he didn't feel like hitting something, he'd almost be able to laugh at the irony of the situation. For over a month she'd been his and he hadn't appreciated her hadn't understood exactly how freaking lucky he'd gotten when those baggage handlers had gone on strike and he'd been trapped in a car with her. And now he knew, and it was over. She was walking away.

Images flashed across his mind: Poppy smiling at him sleepily when she opened her eyes first thing in the morning; Poppy giving herself a shampoo Mohawk in the shower and insisting that he have one, too; Poppy standing in his kitchen, folding pizza boxes for recycling and reprimanding him for his crappy eating habits.

For five years he'd been sandbagged inside his own life, too exhausted, too goddamned weary and wary to risk feeling anything for anyone. Then he'd met Poppy, and she'd burned her way into his heart with her warmth and her spirit.

He stood.

"No way is this over. No freaking way."

He grabbed his car keys and headed for the door.

11

Poppy made it around the corner from Jake's apartment before she had to pull over. The ache in her chest was so painful she rubbed the heel of her hand over her sternum, over and over. Tears slid down her face.

She'd done it. And she'd done it without crying or breaking down and asking him if he loved her or felt anything for her beyond desire. A small victory, but an important one.

She stared out the windshield of her car. Who was she kidding? There was no upside to this situation. She'd fallen in love with a man who wasn't interested in anything other than sex. She'd done it with her eyes wide-open, telling herself every step of the way that she could handle it, that she was in control.

Hah.

She was so tired. She'd had a terrible night tossing and turning then finally pacing as she came to the inevitable, painful conclusion that she needed to end things with Jake.

She kept thinking of the previous day, the moment when she'd understood that he'd celebrated his birthday without her. She'd let him into her heart and her life, confided her fears, cried out her grief, shared her secrets. And he hadn't even been able to let her know it was his *birthday,* or that his family were in town to celebrate it. That was how little she meant to him. How compartmentalized she was in his life—Poppy Birmingham, slotted neatly away in the pigeonhole marked "sex, when you like it, how you like it, no strings attached."

Well, not anymore.

Poppy took a deep, shuddering breath and started the car again. She knew that on one level it was unfair of her to be angry with Jake. He hadn't promised her anything, after all. Not a single word regarding the future, his feelings, their relationship had ever passed his lips. In fact, he'd warned her that he was a poor prospect, that he didn't want to settle down or commit. Yet their relationship had quickly gone beyond the bounds of what anyone would define as casual. It had become intense and all-consuming and both of them had been a party to that. Except she was pretty sure she'd have to hold a gun to Jake's head before he admitted as much. God forbid he ever trust someone enough to talk about his feelings. God forbid he ever let his guard down for one second.

She made an impatient noise as she signaled and turned onto her street. She was hurt, and she was angry with him for being so damn stubborn and obtuse and disinterested that he'd let that happen, but she also knew that Jake couldn't help being the way he was. He was damaged. Someone—his ex-wife, probably, but how would Poppy know since he hadn't seen fit to confide in her?—had hurt him and he was determined not to let the same thing happen again. It was a pity she hadn't understood all of that before she'd lost her heart to him.

She thought she was going home until she found herself turning into the parking lot at the pool. She smiled a little grimly as she grabbed her swim bag from the backseat. It wasn't as though she had anywhere else to go to seek comfort. Uncle Charlie was gone, and her parents had never been her confidantes.

She changed into her swimsuit with brisk economy. The fast lane was empty when she made her way to the outdoor pool. She performed a racing start even though she hadn't taken the time to warm up, exploding out of the block with everything she had. The water rose up to meet her and she closed her eyes for a second as she felt its familiar, all-encompassing embrace. She started to swim, powering up the pool with a length-eating freestyle stroke. The end of the lane arrived quickly and she did a tumble turn, surging away from the wall. Her shoulders were tense, her stroke choppy. If Uncle Charlie or her coach were watching, they'd tell her she needed to pace herself, that she'd burn out well before the race was done.

She didn't care. She wanted to not feel and not hurt and the only way she knew how was to push herself to the limit. She swam faster and faster, her muscles screaming, her lungs on fire. And then somehow she was swimming and crying at the same time and she was swallowing water and choking. She stopped midstroke, reaching blindly for the line-marker. The plastic dug into her armpits as she threw her arms over it and tried to breathe.

It hurt. It physically hurt to love Jake Stevens and know he didn't love her back.

For the first time in her life, the pool failed to offer the sanctuary she craved. Go figure. Just when she needed it the most, the comfort of the familiar deserted her.

Her arms and legs heavy, she swam slowly to the end of the pool. It wasn't until she'd pulled herself up the ladder that she saw Jake waiting for her where she'd left her towel on the bleachers. She stiffened, wondering how much he'd seen. Her thrashing up and down the pool? Her crying and holding the lane marker?

She squared her shoulders. It didn't matter. She felt the way she felt. There wasn't anything she could do about it, and it suddenly seemed supremely foolish to pretend she didn't care. Besides, telling Jake she loved him was probably the one surefire way to get him to keep his distance.

Face set, she walked toward him.

SHE'D BEEN CRYING. Jake fought the urge to haul Poppy into his arms and instead offered her her towel.

"Can we talk?" he asked as she patted her face dry.

"Why?"

"Because I want to know what happened. Why one minute we were okay, and then the next you were gone."

"There is no *we*. There never has been." She pushed past him and walked toward the change rooms.

"That's bullshit, Poppy. We've practically lived in each other's pockets for the past month. What the hell was that about?"

"Sex, apparently."

He grabbed her elbow before she could disappear inside the women's change room.

"You can't bail on me like this. At the very least I deserve an explanation," he said, fear and confusion getting the better of him. She was so adamant, so damned determined.

What on earth had happened?

She stiffened then jerked her arm away from him. "Why should I tell you anything about how I'm feeling or what I'm thinking? Why should I bare my freaking soul to you when you can't even bother to let me know it's your *birthday?*"

He stared at her, the pieces falling into place. Damn. It hadn't even occurred to him.

He almost laughed with relief as he understood why she was upset. This he could fix. Definitely.

"My family surprised me, Poppy. They turned up on my doorstep Saturday afternoon. I had no idea they were coming over from Adelaide. I swear, if I'd known, you would have been there," he said.

He reached for her, needing to touch her, but she took a step away from him.

"So you had no idea it was your birthday? Is that what you're telling me?"

He frowned. "It wasn't exactly a red-letter celebration, Poppy. I'm thirty-six. It's no big deal."

"You don't get it, do you? You know everything about me. You've met my sister and my parents, you know about Uncle Charlie. You know how hard it's been for me to adjust to working at the paper. You know I'm messy and that before I met you I had no idea about sex. I've cried on your goddamned shoulder, Jake. And you can't even tell me it's your birthday."

"Poppy…"

"No. No more. I'm sick of being on the outside of your life. I'm sick of being someone you sleep with but don't share with. I deserve more."

"You're not on the outside of my life. Not by a long shot. There's no one else but you, Poppy."

"If that's true, then what happened the night you sent me home, Jake? What made you so upset that you couldn't stand being near me?"

He stared at her. His past with Marly had nothing to do with this. Poppy was a clean slate, a fresh start. He didn't want any of the past clinging to his future.

"It was nothing to do with you, I swear it," he said.

"See? You don't trust me. You can't even tell me that you've started writing your next book. You think I don't notice when you shut me out, Jake? You think it doesn't mean anything?" Her face crumpled for a moment. She pressed her fingers against her closed eyes, took a deep breath as she tried to regain control.

He couldn't stand seeing her like this. He pulled her into his arms. Her body felt cold against his chest.

"Poppy. Please," he said. He wasn't sure what he was asking for.

She rested her forehead against his chest for a few seconds, then she pushed away from him, shaking her head.

"No. I can't live like this. I can't give you all of me and accept a part of you. I can't love you and take the crumbs from your table."

He stilled. Poppy loved him? He closed his eyes. Of course Poppy loved him. He was the biggest freaking idiot under the sun.

When he opened his eyes again, she was about to disappear into the change rooms.

"Wait!"

"There's nothing more to say, Jake," she said sadly.

She turned the corner. He lunged after her, only to pull up short when a middle-aged woman and her grandchildren emerged from the change rooms. The woman gave him an outraged look.

"This is women only!" she said.

"Sorry," Jake said, grinding his teeth with impatience.

He needed to go after Poppy, to explain to her that he loved her, too. He needed to convince her that he did trust her, that the only reason he hadn't told her about Marly and the baby and all that mess was because it didn't matter. It wasn't a part of his life anymore. As for his writing... Surely once he'd explained that it wasn't a book he was working on, that he didn't really know what it was himself, she'd understand why he hadn't mentioned it, why he'd kept it so close to his chest?

Jake closed his eyes as he realized what he was doing: making excuses, coming up with ways to convince her to give him another chance on his terms.

She was right. He'd shut her out.

He'd been so busy fooling himself he wasn't falling in love with her. He'd given ground by slow degrees—first admitting he found her desirable, then giving in to the need to spend more time with her, get to know her. And all the while he'd been quarantining the parts of himself that held his saddest, ugliest truths.

He remembered something his mother said last night: *the look in your eyes, the way you carry yourself—it's as though you're always braced, ready to defend yourself in case someone gets too close.*

Loving Marly had just about finished him. She'd needed so much from him, been so vulnerable. By the time it was over, he'd been empty. Exhausted. Loving someone who was in so much pain and being unable to help her had been the hardest, saddest thing he'd ever done. He'd been determined to never, ever put himself in a position of caring that much again. Of being that vulnerable.

But Poppy was not Marly. She was her own person. Strong, determined, disciplined. Funny, wise, honest. He loved her. Irrevocably. Even though he'd resisted his feelings every step of the way.

And he'd hurt her, time after time.

He ran his hand over his face, thinking of all the times he'd kept her at arm's length. She was right—she deserved more. She deserved everything he had to give.

He started walking.

Suddenly he knew exactly what he needed to do to make things right.

IT WAS NEARLY DARK by the time Poppy returned to her apartment. She'd been reluctant to go home after her swim, afraid that Jake would be there waiting for her, so she'd driven into the city and drifted through the shops. She didn't want to face him again, not today. It would be bad enough tomorrow and for all the days after tomorrow when she'd have to work with him and try not to blubber every time she saw him.

Her steps slowed when she approached her front door. Jake was sitting there, his head leaning against the door. His eyes opened when he heard her and he stood.

"I wanted to give you this," he said.

For the first time she saw that he had a sheaf of papers in his hand.

"This is what I've been working on," he said. "It's not a new book, it's something else. A record, maybe. Of my marriage. Of what went wrong."

She stared at him.

"Will you read it?" he asked.

"If that's what you want."

"It is." He frowned, looked away for a moment. "It's pretty sad and small, but it's what happened. It's part of me. And I want you to know." His voice was thick with emotion.

"Jake—"

"There's more, but it can wait," he said. "I know I've hurt you, Poppy. I'm more sorry than you'll ever know. But I want to try and make it up to you."

He handed her the papers then turned away. Poppy opened

her mouth to call him back, but then she glanced down at the
top page of his story.

> He wasn't sure when it ended. It wasn't as though a light
> switched on or off inside him, or he woke one day and
> the world had changed. It just…happened. She was still
> his wife. He still loved her. But it hurt him to look at her
> sometimes. So much pain. Leaking out of her, all the
> time. And he'd run out of fingers to plug the holes….

When she looked up again, Jake was gone. She stood
frozen for a moment, half-afraid of what she held in her hands.
Then she unlocked her front door and entered her apartment.
She shed her coat and sat at the dining room table, Jake's story
in front of her. She smoothed her hands over the crisp white
pages with their neat lines of print.

A record, he'd called it. He wanted her to know.

It felt like a huge step forward. It felt like everything.

Lowering her head, she started to read.

It took her nearly three hours to reach the final page. She
felt drained. She pushed the manuscript away from herself
and used the sleeve of her sweatshirt to wipe the tears from her
face.

As Jake had said, it was small and sad, the kind of everyday tragedy that happened to many, many people. The loss of
a much-anticipated baby. Marly's subsequent depression.
Jake's guilt for being on a book tour when it happened. The
counseling. The terrible day when he came home from work
to find Marly unconscious in the bathroom, an empty bottle
of sleeping tablets beside her. Her first words on waking:
hate you. Jake's pain and rage and guilt and love and hate.

It was all there, captured as only Jake could capture it—

honestly, vividly, emotionally. It made her want to howl for him. And it helped her understand.

Why he'd locked himself away. Why he'd denied what was happening between them. And how much it must have cost him to hand over his intensely personal, revealing story to her.

She reached for a tissue and blew her nose. Then she grabbed her car keys and headed for the door. Her feet were a blur on the stairs and she broke into a run as she exited her building. She needed to see him, right now. She needed to tell him—

"Poppy."

She stopped in her tracks. Jake was leaning against her car, his arms crossed over his chest. He straightened, arms dropping to his sides. She frowned, then she understood: he'd waited for her. He'd hand-delivered his story and waited out front of her apartment in the dark for three hours while she read it.

She walked toward him. He met her halfway.

"I'm sorry," she said.

He shook his head. "You don't need to apologize to me."

"I'm not. I'm just sorry." She reached out and cupped his face. "I know it must have been incredibly hard for you to let me read this."

"I trust you, Poppy. I never didn't trust you. I think it was myself I didn't trust."

"It doesn't matter."

"It does. I pushed you away so many times. You're the best thing that has ever happened to me and I almost lost you."

"It doesn't matter."

To prove it to him, she pressed a kiss to his mouth. She broke the kiss and rested her cheek against his, her hand still cupping the side of his jaw.

"I love you, Jake."

His hand came up to hold her face and they stood cheek to cheek, holding one another close for long moments.

"I love you, too, Poppy. More than I can say."

She closed her eyes. It was nice to hear the words at last, but she didn't need them. Not now.

Jake's hand slid from her cheek, and he wrapped both arms around her and held her so tightly it almost hurt. He pressed his face into her neck and she could hear him breathing, struggling for control.

"Thank you," he said, his voice muffled. "Thank you for giving me another chance."

He was crying. She held him tightly, fiercely. She'd wanted to share his pain, and here it was. She closed her eyes, pulled him closer.

"I'm not going anywhere," she said quietly. "I love you and I'm not going anywhere and no matter what happens we'll always work it out."

He pulled back so he could look into her face. Her heart squeezed in her chest as she looked into his eyes. There was so much raw vulnerability there, and so much determination. And, finally, at last, so much love.

"Poppy Birmingham, you are the most amazing person I've ever met. Freaking courageous. So bloody determined you put me to shame. Sexy as all get out." He shook his head, made a frustrated noise. "There are no words. I adore you. I don't know what I did to deserve you, but I've got you and I'm not letting you go."

"No words, my ass."

He smiled. Then he looked into her eyes and the smile slowly faded.

"Forgive me for being the stupidest man on the planet?"

"Careful. You're talking about the man I love."

"Poppy."

She kissed him. "We both made mistakes. Ever heard the saying it takes two to tango?"

"You're always letting me off the hook."

"I know. Kind of makes you wonder what's in it for me, doesn't it?"

As she'd hoped, he laughed. Then he slid his hand into hers and began to lead her up the path toward her apartment.

"Where are we going?" she asked, even though she knew. It had been a whole twenty-four hours since they'd been naked, after all.

"I'm going to show you what's in it for you. It may take a while. How does fifty or sixty years sound?"

He glanced at her over his shoulder. Warmth unfolded in her chest at the look in his eyes.

"Wow. That's a lot of showing. You sure you're up to it?"

"The question is, are you?"

She was grinning. She couldn't help herself. Jake loved her. He'd let her in, finally.

He smiled back at her and used their joined hands to tug her close.

"Answer the question, Birmingham," he said, his mouth just inches from her own.

"Yes," she said. "Yes. Yes to the moon. Yes to infinity. Yes."

He smiled into her face.

"Correct answer."

*Bestselling author Lynne Graham is back
with a fabulous new trilogy!*

PREGNANT BRIDES

Three ordinary girls—naive, but also honest and plucky…

*Three fabulously wealthy, impossibly handsome
and very ruthless men…*

*When opposites attract and passion leads to pregnancy…
it can only mean marriage!*

*Available next month from Harlequin Presents®:
the first installment*

DESERT PRINCE, BRIDE OF INNOCENCE

* * *

'THIS EVENING I'm flying to New York for two weeks,'
Jasim imparted with a casualness that made her heart sink
like a stone. 'That's why I had you brought here. I own this
apartment and you'll be comfortable here while I'm abroad.'

'I can afford my own accommodation although I may not
need it for long. I'll have another job by the time you
get back—'

Jasim released a slightly harsh laugh. 'There's no need for
you to look for another position. How would I ever see you?
Don't you understand what I'm offering you?'

Elinor stood very still. 'No, I must be incredibly thick
because I haven't quite worked out yet what you're offering
me.…'

His charismatic smile slashed his lean dark visage.
'Naturally, I want to take care of you.…'

'No, thanks.' Elinor forced a smile and mentally willed him not to demean her with some sordid proposition. 'The only man who will ever take *care* of me with my agreement will be my husband. I'm willing to wait for you to come back but I'm not willing to be kept by you. I'm a very independent woman and what I give, I give freely.'

Jasim frowned. 'You make it all sound so serious.'

'What happened between us last night left pure chaos in its wake. Right now, I don't know whether I'm on my head or my heels. I'll stay for a while because I have nowhere else to go in the short term. So maybe it's good that you'll be away for a while.'

Jasim pulled out his wallet to extract a card. 'My private number,' he told her, presenting her with it as though it was a precious gift, which indeed it was. Many women would have done just about anything to gain access to that direct hotline to him, but his staff guarded his privacy with scrupulous care.

Before he could close the wallet, his blood ran cold in his veins. How could he have made such a serious oversight? What if he had got her pregnant? He knew that an unplanned pregnancy would engulf his life like an avalanche, crush his freedom and suffocate him. He barely stilled a shudder at the threat of such an outcome and thought how ironic it was that what his older brother had longed and prayed for to secure the line to the throne should strike Jasim as an absolute disaster....

* * *

What will proud Prince Jasim do if Elinor is expecting his royal baby? Perhaps an arranged marriage is the only solution! But will Elinor agree? Find out in DESERT PRINCE, BRIDE OF INNOCENCE by Lynne Graham [#2884], available from Harlequin Presents® in January 2010.

REQUEST YOUR FREE BOOKS!

2 FREE NOVELS PLUS 2 FREE GIFTS!

HARLEQUIN®

Blaze™

Red-hot reads!

HB10

HARLEQUIN® *Blaze*™

*It all started
with a few naughty books....*

As a member of the Red Tote Book Club,
Carol Snow has been studying works of
classic erotic literature…but Carol doesn't
believe in love…or marriage. It's going to take
another kind of classic—Charles Dickens's
A Christmas Carol—and a little otherworldly
persuasion to convince her to go after her
own sexily ever after.

Cuddle up with

Her Sexy Valentine

by STEPHANIE BOND

Available February 2010

---

red-hot reads